A Masquerade
of Sorts

I

A Masquerade of Sorts by Shane Goulette. Copyright ©
2018 by Shane Goulette.

AKNOWLEDGEMENTS

The author would thank to thank anyone who is reading
this bit of literary trash. You have bad taste; it's ok, we all
do. As with anything the author has been influenced by
the pantheon of characters displayed in his various quips
and anecdotes. Rabble Rabble. There is a thanks should
ring a thousand times for everything need happen for this
book to be written; the author would like to express his
gratitude towards all of them.

Cover art © by Chase Rowell

III

Caitlyn, this one is for you.

FORWARD

"All right, all right," Hank went on, "shut the fuck up, seriously," they had all been drinking of course, "Ben, sshshsh, Shut the fuck up."

"Hank you are toast."

"No, shut the fuck up. Shut the fuck up," he waved his hands around, clearing the air, "Ben."

"Yes," Ben sat across from Hank, asian-style coffee table between them.

Hank lit a cigarette, "you never asked me."

"What?"

"You asked all of them, you know, why they do this? Me, now you left me out. Can I ask you why?"

"I just assumed it was because you had the money, so why not? I never really read in to it. Bird over there, and Hitch, I didn't know…."

"I do it because I'm crazy," Hitch cut in, "certifiably ill."

They all laughed, ceiling fan spinning above. Hitch got busy breaking up a cigarillo in to the trash.

"Seriously," Hank would not let up, "is that why you never asked me?"

"Tell you the truth Hank, I don't really give a fuck."

"Listen to this one," the one they called Bird sat on his own chair, right by the window. He closed the drapes, "such the temper. I told him not to ask, you narcissistic fuck." Bird laughed, tilting back his chair, "you have enemies from here to Wichita, Hank. Your alter ego probably does, too."

"I do like the away games," Hank stood up, "I love it when people think they have an advantage on me." He reached and pulled a mask from his face, exposing quite the squared and handsome features. The other's had already shaken off their gear, it was strewn about, various artworks stared at them from the walls, music thumped through speakers. "I mean the beginning, at least the beginning of this," Hank said, "for me."
Hitch chuckled while he tried wetting the blunt, rolling it around, "this is a good one, tell it Hank." Hitch found his lighter, bringing it to the now re-wrapped cigarillo, inhaling.

"So, what, eight years ago. I would have been sixteen, parents had just died, left me a king's ransom, yadayada. Look, I've never had true contempt for the, how we say, illegal lifestyle. My parents died of cancer. No one I love besides your father has ever been murdered," he nodded to Ben, who sitting there must have been only nineteen himself, "the Merchoni family, Ben, do you remember them? Your dad ever say anything about them?"

"No," Ben said, "my dad never told me about that, he never really said much about anything."

"Ah, well they were the first big job I ever did with him and Hitch. Bird wasn't with us yet. Like I said I was sixteen. I must have two billion dollars at my disposal right now so you can only imagine how much it was when I had just gotten it; Salvador Merchoni invited me to his eldest daughter's wedding, even gave me a gift, for my parents' passing," Hank took the blunt from Hitch, dragged, tried keeping his chuckles to himself, "his fucking wife came on to me in the bathroom and I fucked her."

"Wait,"

"Yeah, sixteen, which is technically statchetory, I guess. But I'm a big guy now and I was then, too, you know. Shit I helped take down all of his empire later that year."

"Hank," Bird said, asking for the smoke.

"Sorry," passing it on, realigning his thoughts, "while I was fucking his wife I heard that fucking fuck Sal Merchoni murder someone. At a fucking wedding! What's wrong with the guy! Of course someone was going to see!"

"Jesus,"

"Yeah, so I was just in there, like MILF fantasy fulfilled, she told me I had a bigger dick than her husband," he laughed, "chicks just say that shit tho, but not to guys with small dicks. Even if it's a little above average it's admirable and girls like to point it out, i've noticed. It's nice, you know?"

"You digress, okay,"

The blunt keeps rolling around, fog growing heavy, Hitch gives it back to Hank, the room around them barely noticeable as the smoke spot in Hitch's hideout: couched, comfortably furnished with pillows, speakers, statues of buddah; it was sanctuary.

"We were really just going at it for probably a half hour. I had a joint on me and she sucked my dick after I let her smoke it. When I was talking to the don he joked and said she hadn't fathered any of his kids and that she was, 'tighter than a crevice in a river, and wetter than one, too,' and I'd call that an accurate assessment. Granted I've always been…." Hank waved at his balls, "gifted, but she was good. Right in the middle of it I hear these guys come in, shouting. I was still inside her and when he spoke she looked at me and I knew it: don't say a word, hope we don't get found." He coughed, "I have to tell you I never fucking felt so alive in my life. Moments from death….we heard the gun go off, something about a 'debt that was owed,' as with anything, right? Jesus, the crematoriums hand out bills. Hitch, would you like to interject?"

Hitched kicked the idea around, you could see him playing a mental game of futbol, "we were hot on Merchoni, the guy he killed was a friend. Merchoni found out. We're lucky Merchoni only killed him, had he even tried torture that fat fuck would have rolled on us. This could have been an entirely different story."

"And it may have," Hank went on, grinning, "I moaned,"

"what?"

"You know, I was already inside of her and we had to be quiet, her husband was yelling at this guy, outside of the stall. She moved her hips a bit and it felt good. I moaned just before Merchoni shot the guy. There was a brief moment I thought, 'well this is okay he couldn't have heard that; there was a gunshot,' but then he said, 'did youse guys here that?' and I knew I was fucked. Then she moved her hips again and *she* moaned, that sick fucking broad. I booked it before he could find us, over the stall. The door was close. They were a lot quicker than I thought they'd be, being fat italian guys, tho I had them beat. Anyway, he knew it was me so he kept sending guys to my house, I was always having to move around because people were always trying to kill me. What's fucked up is that I never was planning on going to the cops. I didn't give a shit. But his wife said I raped her so obviously he had more than one chicken to fry with me. He tried paying people off to come at me but he didn't have enough. One day his wife came forward and admitted that she had, in fact, seduced me and he lost it. Started going after everyone, killing cops, whoever he had to do in, just to get to me. Anyway I met Hitch, as well as your dad, one night. I was out drinking, walking home by myself. This was when I lived in that loft downtown, a few streets from here."

"Those were the glory days," Hitch laughed to himself, cutting in, "your dad and I used to beat on muggers, assholes, anyone we could. Back then people weren't scared of doing shit like that. Over the years we've scared that kind of shit out of them. That first year we must have beat two or three a night. Word spread."

X

"Everything evolved, too. It still is, I just hope I have enough money to be ahead of it. When word got out about Hitch and Buck, muggers armed themselves better, and so on." Hank sighed, "we create these things only after we destroy them. If darwinism is true then maybe we are not completely evolved, there are still some things we have to weed out. It all takes time. They were beating on a guy who was pumping his little weenie in to an unconscious woman. I deduced it as I approached. I saw them beating on him and stopped, watched. They were really taking it to this guy. I asked how much for personal protection and we got to talking. I was public enemy number one to a certain faction of a crime syndicate and so too did they want to be. I laughed, they wanted in so bad. I thought it all a joke until we fucked them in to oblivion. Hitch and your dad must have trained three times a day for a decade, the kind of shape they were in, like NAVY SEALS on blow. I realized how much it would actually take to knock me down, and it felt good. I trained with Hitch and Buck for three months, then paid for us all to go train for six-months near songful foot-hills in China, or somewhere in east Asia. Then we came back, backhanded the Merchoni family and paid for all this fancy shit just so it could kill your dad. We'll all be lucky to see thirty-five." Hank reached for a bottle now, pouring four shots. "Either that or we'll all be just fine, Ben." He extended the glasses, "who's to know? Drink up."

1.

Down State street there is Argon Lane. The Trident City Police force often find themselves called to various scenes on Argon. Also down Argon is a man named Marcus Slaughter, a.k.a. Marcus Slaughter, rapper. The sun was well up when he awoke. Two feet to the floor next his bed, he was a new man again. The depression would be gone until he missed being under again.

"Zee." Marcus said, walking out of his bedroom, noticing Zee with his eyes open--Zee, his DJ, was lying with some girl Marcus did not recognize. "Did ya'll fuck on my couch?" Marcus asked.

"Yeah." Zee said. "But I got everything dry-cleaned. This couch is cleaner than Shaneesha's asshole."

"I just got it bleached." Shaneesha sounded boastful, proud of this fact.

"Did you put bleach on my couch?"

"You're missing the point." Zee said, rolling up the sleeves on his jacket; it was the top half to a sweatsuit. "Not only is she clean, I'm clean and so is your couch. Why don't you chill the fuck out or go take one of them long ass naps you just woke up from. What, I'm just supposed to sit here and NOT be attracted to her sexually?" She half-blushed as he finished the words. She was buxom, tho Zee was somewhat of a bear himself. She had a nice enough face and lips that felt good on the dick. She also housed a veritable plethora of diseases in her cunt. Some cunt.

"I don't even know who this bitch is. Who are you, bitch? Why are you in my house?"

"I'm Shaneesha."

1

"Shaneesha, get you and your devil-like ways off my couch and out my house."

"I can't."

"Why not?"

"Oh yeah I've been meaning to ask you, man. Can I borrow fifty bucks?" Zee bud in.

"Fifty?" Shaneesha asked, looking disgusted.

"A-hundered?" Zee sounded meek.

"You're going to have to tell that pimp you're a bit short today." Marcus addressed her.

"Fine. Zee, yo' dick may be the smallest thing on this whole damn planet and you?"

"Marcus."

"Marcus, I'd venture to say you've never satisfied a woman before."

"Bitch, fuck you. Get out my house."

Shaneesha got up, fixing her skirt and strapping in her heels. Her lips still drooped a little below the skirt-line. She was going to walk away but paused for a double-thought; she reached out, slapped Zee in his face, then walked out with the sass and dramatism only a proud black woman could exude.

"Damn what crawled up her snatch and laid a dookie?" Zee asked, hitting his blunt again.

"Probably *yo'* nasty ass dick." Marcus said, chuckling. "Now up, hace pronto, rapido rapido. Get outta here I got shit to do."

"Alright. Oh. Here." Zee extended an envelope to Marcus. "It was on your stoop this morning."

"Thanks. Later days."

Zee left and Marcus opened the letter:

Emcee, we thank you for your interest in joining. You may not be aware, but we have already interviewed you. Your references have been checked. We also took the liberty of making a purchase or two from your weedman. He seems honest and has excellent prices. Please stay in tonight.

Marcus would have been a bit put off had he been a different, more fragile, man.

The letter didn't have any indication as to whom had sent it. But, Marcus knew. He had sent the e-mail reaching out to these people. The heroes were well known in his town. They had helped when natural disaster struck, or when a prostitute's cries for help rang out through the night. They had even managed to catch a serial killer a few years back. That was the only time they had gone on television. Only one of them spoke. They were all in uniform, each unique but still part of the whole. The man who spoke said his name was Hitch. He pointed to his cohorts and introduced them as Birdie, Rye, and Salem.

Now, I want it to be known that we're not (bleep) around. I know most of you would not dream of harming another person. But, for those who do more than just dream about it, know that we will find you. More than likely we will find you right when you think you can't be found.

Marcus had laughed when Hitch dropped the microphone and walked out. Hitch had just held the microphone away from his body and let it go while staring with dead-eyes into the camera. Of course, each member of the group had masks on but Marcus could still see Hitch's brown, determined, eyeballs.

3

Everyone in the crowd seemed to take it seriously except for one of the men on stage. Rye--as Hitch introduced him--was choking back laughter as he walked off. Marcus had thrown his own laughter into his elbow as fast as he could.

After that press conference there was almost no crime in his town for quite some time. It had been nearly impossible for Marcus to get a dime bag over the few months that followed. After a year or so people began feeling more comfortable doing dirty deeds. Marijuana and cocaine avalanched through the streets once again. News of the guardians picking off perverts still made their rounds, but Marcus didn't buy pot from perverts.

2.

Mother-fuck, thought Hank as he awoke. He looked around and realized he was in the drunk tank of the county jail. It was around 1 PM, he knew because of the clock on the wall. He fished a cigarette out of his jacket and lit it.

"No smoking" said the officer at his desk, not even looking away from his newspaper.

"It's not against the law to smoke"

The officer put his own cigarette in his mouth and lit it. "No smoking," he said again, "My wife wears the pants at home and I'll be damned if I'm not the one who wears them around here."

"I appreciate you keeping on your pants, officer, but what has that got to do with me smoking?"

The officer chuckled a little bit, "Fuck you, Hank. Smoke your cigarette."

He had half a joke in his mind. Something about a kinder woman.

But, he kept quiet and puffed on his cigarette. He liked the guy. Sometimes people who appeared to be nut-less simply just didn't care about the little things. He didn't care about anything, and he respected people more as they cared about less.

He sat on the hard wooden bench and remembered the previous night's excursions. Vaguely. He and Hitch had gone out on patrol by themselves. Birdie and Salem had gone to a local club to scout out their newest, would-be, member. Hitch was retiring soon so they had put out an ad for his replacement. Hopefuls were to anonymously e-mail their audition videos to various teachers at the local high school.

Birdie could hack in and download the e-mails. Of course, a teacher's e-mail address was monitored by some form of management, so now the speculation on who was prowling the night turned to a few English teachers, barely in their fifties. The news channels even showed reenactments of old, fat, men in tights and sport jackets fighting off crime. He thought about the irony, the portly police officer sitting outside of the cell.

He remembered breaking up a fight or two and even beating the shit out of a man who--to no one's surprise--had a baggy of night-night pills tucked in his pocket, walking some stumbling bimbo home. He never understood how some women couldn't sense the creeps. The guy who pushed too hard to have a rendezvous at his home usually stuck out like herpes on a man's mouth.

He and Hitch had had a few drinks but nothing that would warrant this loss of memory. He sat there thinking for naught a quarter hour when a face walked into the jailhouse and negotiated a release. The officer looked at the man who was clearly homeless, in need of a shave, shower, perhaps some pants, but still came over and unlocked Hank's cage.

"The man's got the money," is all the deputy said.

Stepping out, Hank flipped a smoke to the officer, winked, and walked out the door with his companion.

"Rye you really creep me out when you wink at other men," a prowler came from around the corner when Hank left, from the shadows. A slender man.

"Anyone can be flattered, Andrew. Daddy can't come in and pick up the kid himself?"

Andrew squinted, his cornrows and JNQO jeans flustered along with him, "There was a sign-out sheet. Stop calling me Andrew. What happened to you last night?"

"I was just about to ask you the same. We were at your place and then….nothing. Andrew."

Andrew was quiet, furious, sauntering.

Hank felt bad, it wasn't right, "I walked out and down your steps. Got about halfway down the block before…"

"Before what?"

Hank double-thought, about a couple things, "fuck, I don't remember. Maybe I wasn't composed. Don't you think it's better if I don't use your name in broad daylight while we walk around the city? Wouldn't you prefer me to say Andrew so as not to draw attention?"

"How about we both just shut the fuck up?"

The two walked a few blocks, cut right on to State Street. Along State there were cars bustling. Restaurants with valet parking seemed to be busy as this brightly-lit weekend afternoon reached its peak. They passed a strip of restaurants and bars and came up on the courthouse. Two stone lions guarded the large rows of steps and an eagle spread his wings above some jumbled up letters. The letters were just above the columns, which were made of stone and loomed large between the ground and the roof of the building. Hank knew the letters meant something, but latin was never a language he took much interest in. They passed the library and a laundromat before coming to a small, almost hidden, street, which they ducked in to. There were a few older Italian style homes. Andrew lived in the upstairs portion of his house, which had three tiny rooms and a bathroom. It was enough for one person, but too little for two. They had to walk around back to reach the stairs.

The pair walked up those stairs and proceeded to Hitch's living space. One of the rooms in Hitch's house had couches, artwork, and a monster set of speakers reaching from floor to ceiling. Hitch never showed anyone the other rooms.

"When did Hec want to go out tonight?" Hank asked.

"You mean Bird?" Hitch looked at Hank quizzically, "10:30, we've got to go visit our new greenie to see if he's up for goin' out with us to do the real dirty work."

"Yeah, well if he's not we're better off dropping him."

"Eh, maybe he'd be all the wiser for not going."

Suddenly Hank remembered something that he had not thought about in years, trying to swat it away.

There's nothing you could have done.

The lie didn't make him feel any better at his core, but the thought was enough to keep his focus on the task at hand. He had to keep some green-ass kid safe from the perils of the underworld. Things had changed since they'd caught that perverted mother fucker: while he prepared to slice open the Turner-girl. That and the Opti incident. Everything had been calm for almost two years. Hank sensed that the group was either getting restless or complacent, trigger-happy or soft. Hitch had a sixth-sense, Hank knew, almost as if he could smell the very thoughts of those around him.

"You hungry?" He asked

"And hungover"

Hank looked the living room over, Hitch walked into the small hallway, leading to his refrigerator. The only white man Hank knew with cornrows. This was the only room Hank ever knew to approach. It was automatic. The speakers were enough to power a drug-addled rave but it were the trinkets that always caught Hank's eye. The entire room was a tribute to the various things Hitch was interested in. Bike gears hung on the wall, meshed with bike chains and old handlebars. A small sculpture of Buddha sat on an incense-burning table underneath two samurai swords, crossed the way swords might be on a pirate's flag. Next to this table was a door. Hank knew a few of the secrets the closet behind it contained. Every once in awhile Hitch would emerge with some tool that was beneficial to either Salem, Birdie, or Hank himself.

"What do you want? I have some ham and…what looks like peanut butter?" Called a voice from the kitchen.

"You got any bread?"

"Rye"

Hank heard an airplane fly overhead, smiled "could you put the ham in between two slices of that?"

"Yeah, I'll throw some of these chips on as well"

"They pickled flavored?"

"Does a bear shit in the woods?"

"Not if he's a circus bear." Hank took a seat on the couch and raised his feet to the edge of the circular coffee table sitting before him. He had an old memory floating around in his brain and this sandwich would be the perfect thing to distract him from this ever-clinging mental bur, forgotten but not completely lost, poking at his skin and giving him gooseflesh.

"One ham on rye" Andrew set a plate full of sandwich down in the table in front of Hank.

"With pickle chips."

3.

Today Ben sat at his father's grave. The afternoon was just beginning to start. Ben had come, as he had for the past three years, to celebrate his father's birthday. With him was the people his father had loved most; Mary Jane and Jack Daniels. As Ben took a puff from his joint and a swig of the hooch he looked at the patch of earth which entombed his father, "Well dad, it looks like we got the gang here all here; Benny, Mary, and Jackie D." Ben proceeded to pour half the bottle of Jack over the earth. He smoked half the joint before he took its butt and shoved it into the ground, letting it burn however the wind blew.

The winds were strange at the cemetery. Truthfully, the winds were strange throughout the entire town. Warm air would blow from the west and battle with the cool air driving off the lake. It made for a wonderful climate in the summer. Anywhere Ben would wander in town he could feel a cool breeze hit his skin just as he would begin to feel how brutally hot the sun could be. If the breeze wasn't enough to keep him cool he could turn north, from anywhere in town, walk a mile, and find his ankles in cold water, as if the center of the lake were ice. He had taken trips to the various islands which were accessible by boat and had never seen any ice but he was convinced that somewhere on Lake Eerie there was a small island of ice floating around; perpetually frozen as the lake would never, truly, get warm enough to turn, in its entirety, from solid to liquid. The lake was an unfrozen glacier.

The headstone loomed. Seagulls flew often, overhead, near the sand, their cawing was a constant. The groundsman left the grass longer in the cemetery, he'd said something once to Ben about the wind, 'meaning more when it rustled the grass out here,' Near the edge of the cemetery there was a dropoff in to the lake below. It was a good fifty foot drop and the cemetery justted out over it just a little. Last year a madam and her gravestone fell in to the lake from the erosion. Kids went there all the time to suicide. 'People who don't know irony would claim that ironic and pat themselves on the balls,' Ben thought, his mind often wandered but not quite enough to shake him from reality. His wandering took place at the furthest depths of his mind. His father's corpse rotted below as he stared at the bright green grass which occupied the space before him. This thought snapped him back. The joint he had planted was now burned down to its filter. Ben got up, left what was remaining of the bottle, and made for his car: a small and old, toy-looking, car that was a bright and ugly blue. He paused, the wind shifted again. Ben looked back over his shoulder and at the grave. The bottle of Jack Daniels had tipped over.

"A bottle in the grave is worth two in the bush," Ben laughed wildly at this. He imagined Mrs. Shelda Maine and Mr. Harold Overjoy, his father's neighbors, rolling with laughter as well. Ben turned and got into his car.

No air-conditioning today, Ben thought rolling down the windows. He took a left out of the cemetery and headed around the elementary school stopsign. The stretch of pavement he was on--which some illiterate city manager with a morbid sense of humor had named Hevens Way--met up with State Street. With a left on State, Ben knew he would be in town in about five minutes. He picked up his cell phone and dialed a few numbers as he took that left.

Ring ring ring

"Hyello"

"Hey, did you get Hank out the tank?"

11

"Yeah, how did you know he was in there?"

"I had a missed call this morning from Trident PD, the holding cell extension."

"That's an odd phone number to have memorized."

"A man with two cocks can do a lot of things."

"Two two-inch pricks should not a bragger make."

Ben laughed, "my dad says hello."

"Nice day for the cemetery. Hank's asleep on the couch, has been for an hour or so. You think you can swing by, take him home? He can't be hanging out here all day."

Ben was approaching the courthouse now,"yeah yeah."

"Ask Hank for some money and go trade your car in, too. We don't need people seeing it come in here."
click.

4.

"Your middle name is Cornelius? Who was your dad, the Duke of Ellington? That's fucked up."

Hector '*Cornelius*' Bridge laughed at the young man who sat before him "Keep your voice down, idiot, I've already gotten yelled at twice this week by Marge about your liberal use of the word cunt"

"Someone's gotta tell that troll looking, frizzy haired, white lady that she's a cunt. You can't or you'll lose your job. She yells at me and I can just start crying and carry on about how I've never met my father."

Hector shifted his focus to the chess board that sat on the table betwixt them. He moved his knight up a few spaces and to the right one, merely a distraction from what he was trying to accomplish on the other side of the board. His opponent pondered, further on down the long cafeteria table sat other children playing poker for candy.

"Theo, it doesn't always have to be you."

"Fuck you, motherfucker," Theo came back at him, grinning. "Cornelius, you can't fool me," he moved a piece to the side Hector was trying to distract from.

Shit. The gymnasium was dank, green. The basketball court was too small, ripened banana brown-yellow. It hit the young mentor like a wall but then immediately disappeared: the sadness. Who crawls out of these holes?

Hector had started volunteering at the local community center when Marge, who ran the show, noticed his knack for molding young minds. She hired him not 6 months after he started volunteering to be a permanent daddy-figure. Hector always managed to draw the kids who were smart. Unfortunately, on

13

the side of town Theo was from the smart kids usually ended up dead. They had no allegiance to any gang or club because, well, they were smarter than getting involved with that crowd. But, in Theo's neighborhood, if a kid had no one to watch his back, he was like bread crumbs to seagulls. Theo thought he was one of these bread crumbs; he was completely oblivious of his allies.

5.

Marcus awoke, abruptly. He must have dozed off while he was watching cable. Lucid dreams were every other time he rested his eyes. Realizing his surroundings were not at all real, coupled with the existential whatthefuck of being aware in a dream left him shakey, filled with helium. The first time it happened a car was approaching him and was about to make Marcus-meat on the road. A sudden occurrence happened upon him. He could not get run over. His body was cozy in his bed and he was merely a visitor in his own mind for a few hours. So Marcus, or whoever Marcus was when he dreamt, lied down on the road and bench-pressed the car right into the air, even as it was about to hit him. Another time he had started running only to realize he could go make Paris in a matter of seconds. Time didn't really exist anyway so he could just be there! One time he walked on water, another he'd flown. The more it happened Marcus seemed to realize one thing, once he'd realized the dream it was very difficult to remember where--or how--he had fallen asleep. This led his mind to an immediate freak-out, 'What if I'm driving right now and about to go off a bridge', seemed to be the root of most of Marcus' panic. But, as with anything, focus usually prevailed. Marcus would realize he was in his bed or on a couch with his pen and notebook in hand. However, being someplace that didn't actually exist was always unnerving. Marcus had learned to calm himself in his dreams but, eventually, he would wake up sweating and short of breath, snapped back into reality because his subconscious demanded to remember what reality was.

This particular dream was a strange one. He was at a poker table in a room that was dimly-lit with red bulbs. At the far end of the room there was a door. The table had 5 chairs surrounding it. All but one was occupied by people he must have seen in passing, his mind making up conversations these people might have if they were in a room together. He decided he was supposed to be acting cool. He was playing the kind of guy Kenny Rogers would have been proud of.

You're driving right now, wake up, idiot

Marcus was not driving, but the unnerving had begun. He had just raised the bet when the door at the other end of the room opened. Marcus knew even before the door managed a crack what was on the other side, and immediately froze. What entered was not a man but a dark shadow. What little figure it had was large. The thing moved slowly, if it had eyes it would have been looking directly at Marcus. No one else in the room seemed to notice. Marcus began to fear this thing so he decided he did not want it in his dream. Lucid dreams were funny that way. Once Marcus had control most things were doable. The trick was to completely, and fully, understand that none of it was real. Only then could he jump off a cliff, or change the cards in his hand, as easily as he could scratch his balls when he was awake. The thing didn't waver. It kept creeping slowly toward Marcus in a way that really did frighten him. It was as if the thing knew Marcus could not get rid of it so easily. Marcus tried to wake up but realized he was too petrified to even do that. He was also starting to feel the wave of worry rumble up through him that always accompanied these types of dreams. He knew eventually he would reach his tipping point and wake up in a huff. The thing had crept closer still, curious as Marcus felt himself being pulled back from his subconscious. The thing reached out, but not in rush. Like an old friend who might see him again.

Marcus was now fully awake. He no longer feared the ill-figured shadow. Marcus had become fairly good at not worrying about what his mind did while he slept. He got up, put on his shoes, and walked outside. The sun was low, but there was still a decent amount of daylight to be had. He bopped down the stairs, swung open his gate and entered the street.

Argon was a one-way street which met up with State at one end, and came to an abrupt stop at the other. Marcus' music engineer, Zeek, lived across the street towards the dead-end. He was sitting outside on his porch, smoking. The road soaked in the heat from the sun as Marcus' sneakers pounded on them.

"What's up funky bunch," Zeek did not get up. Marcus approached. Marcus considered telling Zeek about what had transpired that morning but thought better of it. Zeek knew Marcus had applied for the position, something Marcus now regretted telling his beat-man.

Marcus grabbed a basketball, began shooting at the street hoop in the road. He played with lazy swagger and lined up his body well when he shot.

"Did the justice league get back to you yet?"

"Nah"

"Probably for the best. We got too much music to make for you to be fighting crime or whatever those tight wearing fools do."

"They don't wear tights."

"What?"

"I said I wonder if it's easy to fight in tights."

"Probably, hey did you hear about Top's little brother?"

"Who, little Mikey?"

"Yeah, he got shot yesterday. Tried passing off baking soda and laundry soap as cocaine."

17

"So he got shot? He was only what…"

"Twelve, I can't believe that shit. Niggas' brains turn to mush when it gets hot."

"Damn" Marcus said, solemnly. The news both saddened and angered him. His new comrades were probably scouting him out, and because of that, a kid had died. Marcus shook the thought. He wasn't the one who pulled the trigger. Hell, he had nothing to do with the gunshots. Suddenly, Marcus, got a rush of adrenaline and tensed up. Usually he got this feeling right before he tore into a microphone. Pissed off at the idiocy of his neighbors. Pissed off at the morons who decided it was too hard to work for a living and thought it would be easier to sell drugs and shoot people. He'd get so pissed off that he wanted to say fuck music and take a shit all over himself for thinking he was any different from anyone.

"Zeek, let's go. Get that new beat out. Flip it and reverse it. Been watching every nigga on my block from a hearse while they chasing a merceh."

"Lago?" Zeek got into it, lighting the fire.

"or was it a 9-11? from a peasant eatin' feasant to a 'pardon me mister bird I'm just in my sevenfourtyseven,' high, growing boeing boners while your moms downs the jose/ sucks me like a lemon."

Not too long after, bass.

6.

Hector locked the door to the community center as he and Theo stood outside. The building had three or four entrances but Marge locked them up when she left. Marge gave Hector a key to the main entrance because she knew he liked to stay a little later with his kid. Every night Hector would lock up and walk Theo home just as the sun sunk. It was a magnificent evening. The sky was both orange and purple and the clouds rolled above him like an upside-down mountain. Hector was certain that if he were on mushrooms the mountain would look real enough to ascend, conquer. Towards the horizon the mountain broke apart until the clouds were wispy strings of cigarette smoke. Like one of those maps that would bunch lines close together to show elevation and spread when the flatlands bore in.

Theo wiped his nose, the two walked down Green, took a left on State, towards Argon. Most of the walk was silent. Hector was still wondering what the hell happened in that chess game. A few moves after his ill-attempted distraction Theo had set up his bishops and his queen to trap Hector's king in an imaginary box. After the loss Theo had told Hector how a classmate of his had been absent from school that day, Mikey was his name. The principal came in to inform the class that Mike had been shot dead. Rumors circled the classroom. Everything from vampires to suicide had been entertained throughout the day. Theo said he knew what happened. Though, when Hector asked, Theo had recoiled into himself and hadn't said much since.

"He tried selling fake drugs to the wrong guys" Theo said with his head slumped between his shoulders. "It was my idea. We wanted money to get a new video-game."

Hector looked at Theo and was bewildered. He had never thought Theo was the type to try something so foolish. Theo looked like a coward might after running from a fight, his buddy screaming for help before the curb-stomping.

"I didn't mean for anyone to get hurt. I guess I never really thought anyone would hurt someone my age. It was dumb." Theo looked pale, even for a black kid, and would not meet Hector in the eyes. "I'm sorry, I know you expect better from me."

Hector decided now was a good time to break his silence, "I think the problem with expectations is that you're being set up for failure. I can't say that it's alright, because it's not. It was a stupid, stupid, thing to do. But, cliché cliché blah blah. Mistakes happen, the ones with the gravest consequences are the ones you want to make sure you never repeat. Was he like you?"

"What?"

"Smart?"

"No, he had rocks for brains. And I took advantage of it."

Nodding, Hector looked at Theo and could see a few tears rolling down his face. There was nothing left to say. Consoling someone fresh from despair was a fool's errand, folly; everything said would be redundant and go right around the ears. Hector could hear the sound of music thumping through the streets. He spotted the house it was coming from and knew who was inside. A few steps later the music stopped, Hector saw two men come out and sit on the porch. A car with heavily tinted windows crept up and slowly moved along with the two while they continued to walk. The back window rolled down.

"Hey, Theo, what's up boi. Who's this fishscale walkin' you home?"

"Yo' mama's pimp you big lipped fuck-wad." Theo said stopping on the sidewalk. Hector stopped with him.

"You funny, man. Say, I did some cocaine yesterday that I could've used to wash my boxers. You know anything about that?"

Theo began to laugh, "Only that your pea-sized brain doesn't know cocaine from laundry soap. I thought you were some kind of kingpin?"

Hector chuckled a little, he knew the kid had balls, but damn. There were only three guys in the car.

"And what are you laughing at?" the man in the backseat barked at Hector.

"Oh, nothing, I just thought about something Theo said earlier. Something about a cunt or a troll. I don't know. I'm Hector by the way" He said, extending his hand to the car. The man in the backseat paid no attention to it but Hector could see the bewilderment. For a split second he even saw worry,'How could this white-boy not be afraid on this side of town?' The man turned back to Theo.

"We heard the whole thing was your idea."

"It was, I needed money for the new 2k and figured I knew the right shmucks to pull one over on."

"Yeah, well you thought wrong. Say hi to Mikey for us?"

"What?" Theo responded. Hector was surprised how well Theo could hide the fear in his voice.

"When you see him."

Just then the three got out of the car. The man in the back seat was the first to try and hit Theo. Theo dodged the attack and Hector hit the man with a vicious hook shot to the temple.

21

The man fell. The other two occupants of the car were smart enough to realize who the bigger threat was so they both went after Hector. Hector had underestimated these two. He parried and dodged but still, the two kept coming. He landed a blow on one just as one of them snuck a cheap-shot to Hector's nads. Hector curled over in pain but retaliated with an uppercut that knocked one of the aggressors on his ass. Hector saw a flash of light hit his eyes and knew the man who was on Theo had flicked out a knife. Hector tried to get over to him but was held back by one of the assailants, his gut getting socked by the other. Hector managed at using his feet to twist out and roundhouse one of them, sprinting from the other, who was quite large--probably needed a big and tall suit--and ran like a hippopotamus with stiff tree legs. Swinging them from the side of his body like some kind of idiot. Hector began to panic as, at this moment in time, there was no way he'd make it to Theo. The driver went and straddled him, brought the knife to his neck.

"Do it!" The fat one shouted, struggling for breathe. "Stab that little fucker!"

Theo wriggled, reached out to Hector as he tried gaining speed.

Just then a blur shot by, tackling the blade from the driver's hands. After a flurry of punches that were quick enough to make Ali jealous, the mystery man got up. Familiarty sprang to Hector's face, tho he had to stuff it down somewhere, keep it away from everyone else. Hector's two attackers were caught so off guard that they froze. Hector took advantage and knocked the two of them with a quick few punch to kick combos. They ended up on the ground, tho still managed on groaning; Hector gave them a gut check with the tip of his steel-toe boot. The two on the ground tried to grunt but hadn't the diaphragm strength to do so. By now the mystery man, who Hector knew as Marcus Slaughter, was on a knee and talking to Theo.

"You alright, Thee?" Marcus asked, giving Hector the eye.

"Yeah" Theo responded, breathing, kicking the driver as he laid on the ground.

"It looks like your friend here is a honkie"

Hector brought his eyebrows close together, confused. Theo began to chuckle.

"Yeah" Theo said, still chuckling, "crackers crumble honkies rumble."

Marcus responded with a laugh of his own "Man get the fuck home before I adopt your skinny ass and give you everything you ever wanted."

"Just set aside that college fund when you make it." Theo gave Marcus daps, nodded at Hector, picked up his back-pack, and sprinted home.

"You got some balls man. Theo talks about you."

"Yeah"

"You got a nice upper-cut. I'm Marcus, by the way." Marcus extended his hand. Hector placed his own hand in Marcus' and shook.

"I know"

"What?"

"Theo, he's always talking about the rap-star who lives on his street. I've got a few of your mixtapes at my house. I like your wordplay."

"Well, thank you. Shit. You ever seen me at the clubs?"

Hector had been to the local hip-hop joint, "Bop" plenty of times. The place was your typical night-club. Dark, with fancy lighting and laser shows. The dance floor was adjacent to the bar and there was an upstairs that looked over the dance floor and the stage. This was where the VIPs and the talent hung out. Usually Hector hung out at the bar and kept tabs on Marcus to see if he'd make a good addition. Once he had gone purely for pleasure. He had really enjoyed himself.

"I have, actually, you brought the roof down on that place. People love your music." One of the men on the ground groaned and Marcus slapped him with an open palm. Right on his face.

"Alright, well I gotta get back to it. Try not to whoop anyone else on your way home. Come say hi next time you're down at Bop. I'll bring you up to the VIP and show you a good time. I hope you like dark meat."

Hector was inclined, yes, his prerogative was the female, in her entire being; he grinned. "I'll see you around." With that, Hector turned and walked back down Argon towards State. He could feel Marcus watching him, and could almost sense the peculiar look that radiated thereof. Hector had seen Marcus on stage but never up-close. He was a skinnier guy, but tall. The type whose strength could be under-estimated until he bopped you a few times. Just at a glance Hector could tell that even his elbows were vicious. Pointy, boney, he must have been a bitch to box out.

Hector hooked a right on State. It would be another mile or so before he got into town. The sun was giving its last hoorah this fine summer evening as folks in China were probably just beginning to feel its warm rays: waking up to eat rice. Come to think of it, they probably had to make their rice for lunch, as well. Whatever rice they may be making was of no matter to Hector. Night was coming. Hell, it was practically here.

A person can be betrayed by more than just their own face. The shoulder-pads and bullet proof vests, yes plural, would be enough that no one would find Marcus' frame familiar. The weight of his equipment enough to off-set his slight dip when he walked. However, his aura and personality had a weight of their own. Noticeable to anyone who had spent a decent amount of time with him. Hector had only been walking for seven minutes but had already heard three cars whiz by blasting, 'Get Right,' Marcus' anthem to marijuana.

"ROLLIN' BLUNTS IN THE MORNING JUST TO EASE MY SOUL"

Make that four cars

If Marcus couldn't handle it Hector knew they would simply cut-ties. His fellow musketeers wouldn't even reveal their own identities until they were sure of him. Hector had a feeling the kid would handle it casually. After-all, he was already well-versed in using an alter ego on the microphone.

7.

Ben finished his writing for the day just as night began its dark ride. His sentences were crap. His storylines: dismal. Prose uninspired, today was just one of those days. His previous book was now out on the shelves of dollar stores everywhere. He considered how vain it was that he would prowl bookstores to find his works but then remembered he didn't care. He was seventy or so pages into his fourth book and still living off the gratuities from his first. It was a good one, hell any novel about an arborist getting lost in haunted woods probably was. Or at least one about a tree-climber who also had to deal with the ghosts of his slain family.

Everything since then had been crap. He google'd 'prose' to remember what the hell he was even supposed to be doing. His current novella had promise at the beginning but soon flaked out to little more than a long-short story with so much redundancy that he considered offing himself. He labored over a sentence and decided his writing day was done. He'd try again tomorrow. He hated that he had to try. Words were supposed to flow like water through a broken dam. The very notion of an analogy had seemed retarded to him, a symbol or synonym seemed time collapsing and grotesque. Who gave a shit, anyway?

Ben put on his going-out boots and left for Hitch's. All their outfits were stored there. Well, most of the outfit. The actual clothing was there but they had an armory hidden on the roof. They'd leave one by one, and rendezvoused in front of the library or the soup kitchen; wherever they decided would be a good place that night. Generally, they'd meet wherever the homeless did too.

State Street was relatively deserted; it was a Monday night. Ben had pre-ordered a hoagie and picked it up on his way over. He decided on a sandwich that went well with banana peppers, delicious with that oil, vinegar. His sandwich went down faster than feces through a poop-shit; he strut the half-mile between the sandwich shop and Hitch's.

Foot after foot, Benjamin Alvah Paradise trounced on down over the bridge where did bend the river, as well. At the end of the bend and down another road was the park, and Ben could hear it from the bridge, over bouncing from the gorge. He'd played some of his best basketball down there back in highschool, when he'd play with the kids across town.

The pavement was almost perfectly kept up with, very few cracks or rubble. Ben got lost in thought in his walk and suddenly was standing in front of Hitch's. Had he levitated there? Merely thought it hard enough and poof, here he was? Behind everything was the slow hum of insects, Ben went out back, up some stairs, knocked on the door.

"Fuck, Ben, you look terrible. Like a zombie with downs." Hank said as Ben entered the living room. The other two, Hector and Hitch, were sitting on his couch and chairs, already discussing plans for the evening. Hector was going on about how he had ran into Marcus. Based on Hector's account the kid could punch harder than a mule could kick. Unleashing that kind of force on some unsuspecting drunks would be irresponsible. "I'd like to see him fight," said Hitch, "but I'm not sure I want to just tell this kid to beat the shit out of some drunks. Especially if you idiots are picking the drunks. It seems a little like a gang initiation."

"Because it is, Hitch," Hank laughed, "what the fuck man? Is that not what we are?"

"He could have joined a gang if he wanted to, where he's from."

"Jesus Christ, Hitch. Semantics shmemantics. I don't really want him beating up on random people, but I do need to know that he'll do something if asked, or rather, told."

"Do you tell me what to do, Hank?" Ben asked, grabbing a dark black stack of laundry from the floor, changing into it.

"Well, no. But you guys know me. I just want a nice show." Hank put on his mask with a flourish: matte, with eyeholes, a voice modifier by his mouth. The material seemed of tough silk with minimal padding.

"We'll just talk to him about it," Hitch spoke, nodding his head, rolling his eyes, "You need any water, Salem, Rye?"

"Please," Ben said, "that would be great."

Hitch pulled a water bottle from nowhere.

"Remember last year we ended up chasing down that life insurance guy who was killing his clients?" With the voice modulation it was easy to tell the difference between Hank and Rye, who now sounded like a transformer, or some other humanoid robot.

"Yeah he claimed he was helping their families because of the payout."

"Funny what a recession can make a person do."

Once they all had on their spandex and kevlar they smoked a little bit of the hasheesh and left for the library parking lot. Monday night was library night for the homeless. They'd make jungle juice with whatever alcohol they had grabbed during the day. Ben and his cohorts would slip in and meet up amongst them, throwing a bottle of their own into the juice.

It was about a half-hour after the sun had set and the group decided to throw more change in the air and dash over to Marcus'.

Hitch had been playing ping-pong with himself as retirement approached. He would love to step away from it all but he still had so much left undone. Life was not the bitch, hindsight was. As he ran, his body gave him the only answer he may need, aching and leaving him gasping. Keeping pace with fit 20-somethings wasn't going to be in his repertoire much longer. This made him a liability.

The foursome came up to Argon and turned the corner. With a few labored strides they came up to Marcus' home. Pit bulls throughout the street howled to show their displeasure at the intruders. Hitch sprayed something into the air and they quieted.

"Should we knock?" Birdie asked.

"Yes, hello brother. Have you heard the good news of heroism?" Salem had already begun to laugh at his own joke. "Yes, we should knock. I'll sit on the edge of his stoop and look tough and disinterested. Bird, stand against that support beam with your arms crossed."

"Cool, what should I do?" Marcus asked, stepping outside. "Ya'll ain't too sneaky for secret vigilantes."

"Hello Emcee" Hitch said, emerging from behind a shadow, quickly leaving Marcus witless. He nodded to the others who darted away. Marcus would have seen them leave had he not blinked. "My friend has a large mouth. I'm glad to see you stayed in tonight. We stopped by to let you know that you need to put on the contents of this bag and meet us at the east-end of the apartment building behind your house. Don't let anyone see you. I assume you know that anonymity is the name of our game. I hope you prepared catch-phrases." Hitch handed the kid a duffle bag and sprant off on his own.

Hitch took the most direct route and arrived at the rendezvous first. No one was around, but soon he heard the pitter patter of hurried footsteps enclosing around him. Rye emerged from a bush, Birdie from behind, and Salem the street.

They waited for a few minutes in relative silence. With Rye around there never really ever was such a thing. Emcee wandered out of the side entrance and met them.

"Sorry, I thought east was over there."

"It is if you go east enough."

"True shit. What's on the plate tonight?"

Salem took up the answer to this question, "Hazing, man, have you never been initiated into anything before?"

"Initiation 101. We gotta go steal a goat for you to fuck." Hank.

"I thought we were going with a pig this ti.."

"Shut the fuck up you two" Hitch said, quite seriously. "Sure, we made Salem walk with his thumb up his ass but we do that with this guy and it's a hate crime." Hitch didn't often joke, but he wanted to ease this guy in.

"Ah, so I've joined a comedy club. Fantastic."

"One that fights crime, no less, let's get the pleasantries out of the way so we can continue on with our night. Hitch."

"Birdie"

"Salem"

"Rye"

Each extended hands in salutation.

"And I guess I'm Emcee? I mean I thought I was going to get to pick my own name."

"Because all good nicknames come from the people they belong to."

"Damn, dude, you're kind of an asshole."

"Thank you"

"You guys wouldn't even consider letting me use Thunder? Or Rockforce?"

"Not if you don't mind wearing a cape and tights."

This went on for a few minutes as the new member got to know the misfits he now found himself outfitted with. Rye made one too many jokes, Birdie was mostly quiet, Salem put in his wit when the right moment hit, and Hitch sighed. He could tell the kid was double thinking. They were a fun-bunch to the right people, and an idiotic annoyance to most. The conversation eventually reared its head towards what the group called themselves. On the news they had been called everything from the "Dark Defenders" to the "Murdering Menaces". Newspeople had such an affinity for alliteration. In all their years together they had never thought of what to refer to themselves as. They just used their individual codenames and let that be that. Any good nickname was earned. Every pretentious and douchebag ridden group ever gave themselves nicknames. We are the League of Extraordinary Gentleman. Pft. We are the Fantastic Four. How very mickey mouse of a crime fighting organization to call themselves the fantastic anything's. Hello everyone we are the Fantastic Fucktards and we are here to slay a psychopathic murderous villain.

If we continue the story and fast forward all the running involved we may actually get somewhere.

Hitch rolled up his sleeves as he stood at the corner of State and Destin; sexually frustrated family men came here with their hard earned money to get off. Some like ladies. Others, ladies with dicks: without tits, gag re-flex, or legal age—sometimes all four. It was a moral dilemma but our heroes had spent evenings baiting lesters with underage talent, only to wrangle them up. Once a month they'd string up all the molesters by the courthouse so everyone knew who they were. A flash drive stuck to their lapels. A flash drive usually containing all the kiddie porn they'd either made or downloaded. Rye occasionally liked to take a shit on the sick little fucks.

One badly smooth caramel of a woman walked over to the group, she was too hot to touch.

"Monica"

"That's Miss Monica to you, red-beard." Monica said as she smiled, lightly.

"I only call you that in bed." Birdie responded.

"Boy you better grow 5 inches."

"Oooooo, shit bro, Miss Monica bad." Marcus said, choking down the rumble of a thunderous bit of laughter.

"And who is this costumed-up brother with the silky smooth voice?"

"Uh, Emcee." Marcus had forgotten to turn on his voice modulator. Rye reached over, clicked it on, and gave him a thumbs up, winking and making that clicking noise with his tongue.

"Oh yeah, they told me you were coming out tonight. I see why you guys like him. Certainly doesn't look like a bitch." She stopped for a moment and looked them over, thinking. "Everything's pretty quiet tonight. Some white dudes up on Densmore bought half a sheet of acid and a full tube of drops. That could get interesting."

"How many white dudes?"

"Well five or so. Plus one brother. A great big bear of a brother, got Monica all stirred up."

"Emcee, you ever dealt with a man on enough acid to turn his brain to soup?" Hitch asked.

"No"

"Then let's go see what all the hypes about."

The night was cool. If a major league outfielder threw a stone from Destin it would probably land on Densmore. It was a quick jog for Hitch and company. They barged onto the street from different directions. Just a few houses down was a man running around wildly.

"Is that the back end of a golf club?" Emcee asked.

"Where? Oh, sticking out of his ass. So it is. Say, Bird, what kind of club you think is up that man's rectum?" Rye asked, he'd stopped walking and was observing as they all were. Where were the others?

"Seven Iron."

"I'm hoping it's a driver," said Hank, amused with himself. The rest of the gang puckered up and cinched their faces in imaginary pain.

"FOUR!!!" The naked man screamed as he ran in circles, his friends came in to view and appeared to be chasing him: trying to pin him down. You could tell they were all zonked out. One of them latched on to the handle of the golf club and ended up getting dragged around the front yard. The others stopped their pursuit and began laughing slowly and dumbly. Some pointed, others just laid in the grass and rolled around.

"I mean should we do something?" Emcee finally piped up.

33

"Damn I hope that's not a driver," said Birdie, with genuine worry for the man's colon. "Yeah, let's get him to a hospital."

"What about the others?"

"Take whoever doesn't remember his name. Hitch?"

Hitch nodded in approval. They could just call an ambulance, but that would mean cops. Flashing lights and sirens would send all of these kids in to a bad trip, not to mention the general unpleasantness that was dealing with a police officer.

It was acid, not murder.

They devised a plan and set in.

Hitch watched Rye and Em try to round up Golf-Club-Ass. The kid could not be stopped.

"WATER WATER WATER!!!" he screamed as he flopped around in a giant puddle, breaking free of Rye and Em as they tried to grab and pin him down. Birdie and Salem were slapping the others, each just smiled and chuckled. Hitch walked up to the one who was slumped over with his head in hands.

"What's your name?" Hitch asked

The kid smiled, in out of body bliss, "Raaaandy duuuuddee," his words were slow and drawn out.

"You got a car, Rando?"

"Car? Nooooo, I've got a vaaaaan, maan."

"Of course you do" Hitch said as the kid pointed to an old van that was probably made of LSD. As if on cue one of the drugees wandered from the herd Birdie and Salem were watching and began to lick the van, Rye and Em were trying to grab their man while he swung around, bent over, using his club to ward off his pursuers.

34

"WATER, FOUR! WATER, WATER, WATER," he kept shouting over and over. Hitch walked over and slugged the kid in the face. He weebled, he wobbled, but he did not fall down. Instead he put his head down and began to ram into Hitch's stomach. Hitch side-stepped the blow and—quick as a pre-cumming dick—wrapped the guy's neck in his arm on the left side. Rye followed by grabbing the shaft protruding from this man's ass, and got his legs off the ground.

"WATER!" The shouted again as Hitch and Rye carried him to the van. Hitch knew Rye would shout "Four!" as they threw him into it. Sure enough, he did. Birdie and Salem were shepherding their flock over to the van by pointing a couple lasers into it. They shuffled zombilly over with dumb grins and climbed right in to the vehicle. Hitch got in front and began to drive.

"Uhhh, Hitch."

"Yeah"

"I think this kid's kidneys are failing."

"WATER WATER WATER!" The kid screamed again, before making an awful choking and gurgling sound.

"He's seizing up and pissing blood all over."

Hitch turned around in time to see this kid convulsing as blood dripped in his crotch region.

"Salem"

"On it," Salem attached the mouthpiece to his water storing back-pack. He turned the knob and water flowed out.

"Hey stop it," one of the herd said, "oh god what are you doing?" The rest of the herd began to either rock back and forth and scream or get up and rush towards Salem and Birdie, also screaming. Birdie held two of them as one went gungho, adrenaline fueled and stoned out of his fucking mind. It was the great bear of a brother Monica had spoken of. Em hopped the front seat and caught him as he was about to tackle Salem. One in the corner was rocking two and fro, got his lighter out and began to burn the shag carpet encompassing the entire van. The carpet on the floor caught first, then the curtains over the back window, then the ceiling.

"What the fuck is going on back there?" Hitch called, until he looked in the mirror and realized the heat he was feeling. Birdie stomped on the back doors until they gave way, letting the smoke go into the air. A flaming ball of hippie van was probably a strange sight to see barreling down State. If one got a good look they'd see a man inside with blood on his pelvis and a golf club sticking out of his ass. If they looked closer there appeared to be men in costume trying to pull out the club, or shove it in, it was unclear through the smoke. 'WHERE ARE THE COPS??' They'd wonder. Probably sitting on some highway, waiting for someone to go eight miles an hour above the speed limit.

"Shit, shit, shit," Rye screamed as they pulled in to the emergency room turn-around. He was completely turned around in the front seat and had both his hands wrapped around the collars of two hippies who were humming to match the crackle of the flames.

"And only through the cleansing power of the flames can the phoenix rise again," one of those crazy bastards mumbled as he walked towards the fire. Birdie gave him a swift kick in the tookus and he sprang through the ring of fire and landed on the pavement outside the van. Hitch got out as orderlies ran through the automatic doors to come to their assistance.

"Jesus, what happened?" One of them asked.

"Acid" Hitch replied. "The one with the golf club in his ass needs the most attention."

"Yes, I, I think that's fairly obvious."

One of the orderlies brought out a few fire extinguishers and our Dark Defenders put out the van fire and scrammed down an alley before the fuzz had time to get there.

8.

Sometime later and we are found back on Destin. Shadowed drivers pulled up and out, praying to a god they didn't believe in that they weren't taking a cop to some shantied up motel. The hotter a hooker is, the more likely she's a cop. Thus is the paradox of getting a good-looking hooker.

Streetlights were out enough to conceal identity, making everyone have a handsome mystique. There was a bar on the corner. Monica stood outside smoking a cigarette and talking to one of her girls. Hitch noticed the DA walking out of that bar as they walked up.

"Seven Iron!" Hank screamed. Rye gave Birdie a twenty and had the look on his face everyone has when a bet is lost.

Birdie was the first to walk up to Monica. She disengaged from her conversation and walked across the street, towards her overseers. Monica was a broad who knew the value of good protection, especially when all she had to pay was information.

"So?" She said as she leaned on the sign post; 'Destin,' it read.

"We ended up driving a guy with a golf club in his ass to the hospital."

"That's not too bad."

"We drove him there in a van that was on fire, while his kidneys were failing."

"So seven out of ten good night. I haven't heard anything else. Everyone's laying low tonight. The DA and his wife only had one drink at the bar, I don't like it."

Hitch heard thunder rumbling in the distance. Now he didn't like it either. He had told Emcee of the importance of the informant on their way over. "The most important thing," he had said, "is trust. A rouse is an easy enough thing to get caught in."

The six of them discussed what had happened so far in the evening and disembarked. Monica had heard nothing more of interest. She walked down the street to whip some of her girls in to paying more attention to the customer. There was the hum of cars all about, each one prowling to purchase some happy fun time.

On slow nights Hitch would have the group linger around and keep an eye on Monica's girls. However, by now the desperate men who ventured to Destin knew that Hitch and company might be around. This was enough to dispel any inkling of funny business. Cars pulled in, got off, pulled out, and then drove away. Hitch had to find a bigger fish to fry, he didn't want Emcee's first night on the job to be spent peeking into fogged up windows. Luckily, George Hammer was walking out of the bar. Hitch whistled loudly and George walked over to them.

George handled the security contracts for most of the local businesses. He was a portly little chode who could see five moves ahead. The bar was playing its closing time music and George was beginning his half-mile trek home. He was wearing his favorite combination, purple shirt and brown corduroy pants.

"What am I, some kind of dog now? You whistle, I come?"

"Always a pleasure, George." Hitch replied.

"Yeah, yeah, whatever. Where's my treat?" George asked, extending his hand. Hitch put a small sheet into it and George examined the sheet for a second or two, "I haven't seen these bad boys since the seventies, (whistles), how'd you fellas get your hands on these?"

"The guy who had them before didn't really need anymore."

"I'll say, this is some good looking shit, thanks boys." George paused, awaiting some kind of reply. After a few seconds of receiving none he realized something different about the group. "Have there always been five of you?"

"Does a Panama have a canal?"

"What?"

"GEORGE!"

"Oh, right, yeah time is money, money is criminals, yada yada. Gas N' Mart got robbed a few hours ago. Police got the guys. Alarms went off over at Sunset Ridge. Someone in a hoodie broke in and got on the elevator. The only camera that works is pointed at the front door so we don't know where he went. It happened a few hours ago and nothing else really came to fruition so I'm assuming it was just idiocy and anger meeting at the right time."

"Sunset Ridge, the apartment complex?" Birdie asked.

"Yeah, probably just a disgruntled resident. I got nothing else." With that George winked, slipped a tiny strip of acid onto his tongue, and walked down the street. Whistling some obscure—probably made up—tune.

Hitch stood at the corner of State and Destin with no real clue as what to do next. A kid had died last night over by where Emcee lived and Hitch was probably standing right where he was now, and being just as indecisive. Maybe Rye was right, all this non-action had made him soft.

"Alright, Emcee, Rye, you're with me. Salem, Bird, you guys can go on home."

"Nah, I'm sticking with you guys." Salem replied.

"Fine, Bird you're going home."

Birdie departed and went to say a few words to Monica. Our fantastic fucktards began running towards Argon. Hitch wanted to see how well Emcee could blend in where people might recognize him. The night would reach its peak soon and with each, breath quickening, step our heroes were in and out of onlookers' stares. Flashing by so quickly that anyone who caught a glimpse began to second guess their vision.

9.

Monica went by Christine Mathis in the real world. She hated how she had to leave Theo home at night. She often wondered what Theo would think if he knew what she did for 'work'. She didn't think it would bother him, hell, he might even think what it was cool. Christine was a pimp. Granted she didn't wear a fur coat or carry a cane but she did keep her girls in line. She provided housing, food--stamps. Half of the apartments at Sunset Ridge were occupied by them. Regardless, Theo was watched by two different nannies every other night. On their off nights from watching Theo these nannies doubled as Monica's managers for the evening.

Tonight Christine got out her key, unlocked one of her apartments. It was a small place. The only necessities were a bed, a lamp, tall mirror, and full bar. She only used it for one or two things. To her left and her right, the kitchen and the bathroom, respectively. Before her was a small carpeted room: one queen-sized bed, one mirror, one lamp. She veered left and set her keys on the counter-top. Sometimes there were eggs in the fridge. The bar however, which was up above the sink, contained many liquors, given to her as gifts. She poured herself a drink.

KNOCK KNOCK

"Hold on"

KNOCK KNOCK

With a groan, the bottle half-slammed, a slow rolling suspicion snuck on Christine. Wavering through the kitchen, she turned on a few lights, easing her slightly. Why was she so skiddish? It was not unusual, late arrivals.

KNOCK KNOCK

She jumped, laughed eerily. Still uneasy, the peekhole made her anxieties easy enough to solve tho the thought of peering through it filled her very bones with dread. The lights seemed somehow fainter. Christine shook off and sighed, opened her door to find no one in the hallway. The elevator doors to her left opened up but no one shifted in or out. The familiar "hahaha's" of a laugh-track vibrated out of an apartment down the hall and filled the corridor with chortle. She had a silly thought and slyly stole a glance back, tho no one lurked there, her apartment brightly lit. Without looking back into the hallway she shut the door, quickly, shut the lights out. She grabbed her drink, the knife she used to cut lemons, and went to sit on the porch. There were no chairs out there but she sat on the concrete and didn't mind doing so. A cat or two stirred below and the crickets were a full on symphony. Thunder rolled somewhere over the lake, the crickets grew quiet in a unified decrescendo. Christine's ear caught a slight hum that cut through the silence. *Whack.* A three pronged claw grasped onto the patio above her with a suddenness that forced her body to jerk. A lightless blur flew through the air and tumbled onto her patio, dismounting from his zip-line. Christine would have screamed if this were an intruder but instead she laughed as the large costumed man slammed into the wall during his dismount. She immediately ran over to help him up, laughing all the while. The man she helped up to his feet began laughing once he was off of his knees.

"Damn, I really thought I had that."

"You didn't hit it as hard as this time." Christine said through choked laughter. Birdie had been trying to find a sneaky way to get to Christine's room for months. He had yet to find a way that didn't involve him slamming into something. As Birdie pulled Christine towards him she buried herself into his chest and calmed down a bit. She looked up, smiling, and hummed with the crickets. They sounded like children

43

jumping up and down on trampolines. The two sat there for a few minutes. Rocking to some made up tune, clutched close enough to feel the comfort of one another. Christine hummed and worked her hands up to the back of Birdie's head. She fumbled around in his curly red hair for a minute until she found what she was looking for and untied his mask. As she pulled it away Hector Bridge became more and more recognizable. He was still in uniform and his hair looked brilliant with the moon behind it. She could blame the hardness of her nipples on the cool air under her silk dress, but it would be a lie. Hector gave her a once over and Christine could almost hear his dongle harden up. She took off the two or three layers of shirt Hector's uniform contained as he undid the top of her dress. Breasts exposed, she pressed herself against him and carefully kissed his neck. She felt his finger touch her belly button and slide down. She sensed that momentarily he'd want to put his tongue somewhere, too.

"Mary Jane never got it this good," she accidentally said out loud. Hector responded by picking her up underneath her arms and tossing her onto the bed. Christine never recalled taking off her dress but it laid on the floor just the same. The room was dark, tho the moon shone brightly. Light that was sublime seemed to always have a dark edge. But the shadows played beautifully on Christine's soft brown skin. Her nipples like pyramids, she could have been Queen of the Nile.

She played with her lips and Hector crawled towards her in approval. Christine knew what she tasted like; it was no wonder Hector brought his appetite. Christine seized a few times until Hector rose up and playfully slapped her on her nipple. She laughed and covered her breasts.

"Ow," Hector shouted, limply shaking his hand through the air, "those fuckin' things cut me." He glanced up at her and grinned lightly. Christine's laughter became sheer arousal. She was wet enough to take him on so she tackled him and worked slowly down, staring at the porno taking place in her mirror. Hector was broad shouldered and large muscled, Christine herself was broad hipped but skinny waisted. Sex be a diety and that diety be a goddess. A large but not too large breasted immortal with symphonies in her clitoris.

Christine knew some Bach, Schopan.

When the two had finally came some odd few times they laid next to each other, breathing heavily and sharing what was left of Christine's drink. The room seemed brighter, moon slowly filling their retinas. Hector got up to fix a highball. Monica turned over and addressed him.

"So Theo told me what happened today."

"Really?"

"Yeah, did you let him beat you?"

"What?"

"In chess?"

"No, he beats me all the time."

"So do I." Christine jumped from the bed and brought her fist to Hector's side. Hector hit her hand out of the way with ease and, almost simultaneously, brought her up over his shoulder, slapping the ass that now doubled as his second head. Christine squealed and pounded on his back. Hector set her on the countertop and gave her the glass to drink. She did, giddily. Every care that could have crossed her mind suddenly decided on a fantastic vacation.

Time still exists when we are not paying attention to it, ticking down in a slow drum roll towards death. Time is infinite, that's the cruelty of it all. Time gets to keep on going and make our very existence forgettable. Time is the god everyone leaves hanging out to dry. It does not sway, it does not judge.

45

Time does not care what is going on in our lives. It is finite for everything but itself.

The counter-tops even look like something from a dream, seemed infinite in themselves. The cool kitchen tile on Hector's bare feet felt exciting and made him want to dance.

Hector and Christine found their way back in to bed and drank together, laughing at the misfortunes of the day. Conversation soon shifted to what tomorrow might bring. They could say tomorrow held anything and they wouldn't be wrong. Christine's tomorrow always revolved around Theo and his well-being. Hector's tomorrow was currently wrapped in his arms, being enjoyed today.

Conversations that involve two people who are in love are too hard to follow. People actually in love don't lay there and sweet talk each other. One of them farts and the other laughs. The things that are conversed about go off on such wild tangents that following along is nearly impossible to a third party. One minute its pizza rolls, the next its ninja turtles and butt plugs. Cowabunghole!

The butt plugs talk usually leads to some more sex. The sex leads to shower sex. Shower sex turns to bent over the sink sex. Sometimes that leads to balcony sex somehow. Then goodbyes are said, hugs are prolonged. Then, too tired to care about onset loneliness, teeth are brushed and sleep is had.

Christine was in process of brushing her teeth. She would have to leave soon to go home and get some rest before Theo woke for school. She spit into the sink and looked up into the mirror. It was always hard for her to look into a mirror for too long when she was by herself, especially in the dark. The terror of peeking up into the mirror and seeing a face not her own rendered a shudder. She glanced up while she spat into the sink. Braced. Her eyes saw nothing and she shook her head at her own stupidity.

When would someone have gotten in here? She asked herself. She glanced back in the mirror again for reassurance.

Knock Knock

Christine almost jumped then laughed at herself. Though, the knock did sound like it was coming from the inside of the door…

Stop it. It's just those damn kids again.

The lie didn't make her feel any better, at her core, but it was enough to shove the thought from the forefront of her mind.

She went over, electing the peephole. Fear wanted to rape her but she knew it was displaced. On the other side of her door were white walls, a carpet. No psychopaths tonight. She went back to brush her teeth, gooseflesh threatening her arms.

She forced herself to look up into the mirror as she gave her final spit to the sink. Her closet door stood ajar. She only meant to look at the reflection of the door for a moment, knowing it was closed just moments before, but she couldn't take her eyes away. She wanted to, desperately. It was just something her mind could not allow.

Anxiety crushed her innards like a wave that knew how to punch, but she would not waver from looking at that door. The light in her kitchen flickered on and off. Her stove went click*click*click, but was not lit.

"So Theo, and, what'd you call him?" A voice called from the kitchen. Slamming cabinets. "Hector? Or was it Birdie?"

The voice was genuinely curious but also spoke as though it had all the answers. Christine looked down to grab the scissors on her counter and when she looked back up into the mirror a face had appeared both in front and behind her. It peered around the corner from just outside the bathroom and

47

wore a grin that would dishearten even the most righteous of men, eyes darker than any number of terrible things. All seeing, uncaring. Dead.

Before she could scream the napkin slipped to her mouth, and fought as she watched herself go limp with unconsciousness.

9.

The morning light bayed onto the side of a cliff. Twin pillars of rocks begged long-legged immortals climb, waves crashed. Only a truly retarded captain would try navigating them, the cliff, other jagged rocks. Spray painted up some heights where adrenaline-fueled climbers had fallen were initials. Hank's name wasn't on there. All of Trident lay down east.

Building a house on the cliff over Lake Eerie was said to be a bad investment. It would take less than 25 years for the house to slowly dissipate into the waters below. Hank liked the view. He stretched, yawned, rose from his silken sheets. Shades gave way to the light of a new day. A robotic arm reached over, extended a robe. The walls of Hank's bedroom were all glass, he could see the pillars, making way for heaven.

"Trudy"

"What?" an automated voice replied. Artificial intelligence allowed her to sound annoyed at this early of an hour.

"Put 2 eggs and a bagel on Butler's list"

"He will be waking up in five minutes. Would you like coffee or a mimosa?"

"Coffee. Colombian."

"List updated. May I play some music?"

"Does a banana peel?"

"Not by itself, sir."

"Yes, play something."

Some 15 speakers around his room began playing a funky, uptempo song. Nakedly, Hank did a jig in front of his window, easily recognizing the voice on the song.

I use my voice to carry me/ wherever I wanna go/ smokin' blunts in the mornin' just to ease my soul

Hank watched the lake for a few minutes before walking out of his room and into the kitchen. He sat at the island in the center of it and grabbed his coffee from the counter. Around him was everything a chef needed to open a five-star restaurant. This included lots of counter space, stoves, a refrigerator as big as a small apartment, and so much kitchenware that it was almost dizzying. A man emerged from the over-sized fridge carrying three eggs, some cheese, and a bagel.

"Over easy I presume?" the man said.

"Yeah, thank you Butler. Just don't break those yolks."

Butler went over to one of the many stove tops and grabbed a pan.

Hank did not call his butler Butler for no reason. With the amount of money his parents had left him he could afford to do whatever he pleased for multiple lifetimes. So, Hank decided to scour the earth and find a butler whose actual name was Butler.

Breakfast was made and consumed. Newspapers were scoured for any mention of the vigilante known as 'Rye', and weights were lifted. Board meetings were skipped.

What Hank did with his day depended on how hungover he was. If it was anywhere from mildly to extremely he'd rotate between the shower and his bed. If he wasn't at all, like he was right now, his day would be filled with nonsense. One hour would flow into another without him even noticing, mainly because he was usually high on the pot.

Hank was getting out of the shower after his workout. The board would be finishing up right now without him. He'd doubt they missed his lack of presence. He never showed up, and when he did it was usually followed by a prank on all those old bald fucks. He liked that b-holes clenched up whenever he mosied into the boardroom. Sometimes he wouldn't pull a prank and just sit there and grin, watching how uncomfortable everyone would become with anticipation. He had no real interest in running his father's company.

His money was not running out anytime soon. With just one of his CD's he'd make twelve-hundred dollars in the time it took him to jerk off in the shower. One of his twelve hundred CD's. Essentially, his spunk was worth twelve to the second with a few zeroes at the end.

Once he had tried to clean himself up and run the company responsibly. A leaf that turns over is still a leaf.

Knock Knock

"Butler."

"Telling your butler to open the door is a bit redundant, sir." Butler strolled past Hank's room and to the front door.

Hank tucked his towel in at his waist and followed Butler, just a few steps behind when he opened the door. Pinned to it was a small envelope. He quickly reached for it and inside, a memory card. He put it into his phone and opened the only file being stored. It was a video.

For the first few seconds he saw only darkness, then a light flickered on and the room in the video became recognizable. It ought to have. The room that appeared on Hank's phone was the very living room that was behind him, across the foyer and the parlor. A voice spoke but no one was in the room.

"You know, I asked myself 'self, is it possible that the young billionaire with nothing to lose could be a part of this little hero clan?'"

Just then he heard a thud and what sounded like dragging. A man came into the frame. Then another. Hank noticed that the other man, who was being dragged, was himself. The man doing the dragging set Hank down in the middle of the frame. The man spoke to Hank, but to the Hank who lay unconscious on the floor.

"Then I saw all those cool little gadgets, I even saw you jump from a helicopter one time. I'm saying you because of course you were probably the one jumping. Who else can afford to do stuff like that? Who else could afford Kevlar, or a dirt bike with a grappling hook? The answer, I realized, was no one. No one but you."

The man stood over Hank for a moment. He was tall, ape-armed, and wore black pants, boots; he did not wear a shirt. But his skin was black, not like an African but like he was wearing a tattoo or had rolled around in ink.

Hank ran through his memories to try and think of what he might have done to deserve such a visit. Admittedly, he could think of a few instances that warranted this kind of response. However, Hank was sure he had never seen this man before. His hair was long and gangly. He pushed it back and looked over his shoulder at the camera. A smile broke his face. It was an odd smile. Fear wasn't ever exactly in Hank's repertoire but he felt it now. The man bent over, reached for a knife, and made an incision behind Hank's left ear. He lowered himself and cupped Hank's chin in his right hand. He lowered himself even further until he looked unconscious-Hank directly in his shut eyes.

"See you soon." The video went out.

Hank reached up behind his left ear and felt where the man had cut. Sure enough he felt the long, thin, bump that meant his skin was recovering from a flesh wound.

Butler, who was just over his shoulder, said in his most charming of voices, "it appears as though the sleeping dog has been awoken."

"This guy isn't the sleeping dog here, Butler…"

"You are sir, precisely. Clearly you aren't afraid of a man who creeps around your house while you are asleep."

Hank tossed his phone onto the ground and began walking down the corridor to his bedroom, still in towel. "Where the hell were you?" He called back.

"Probably asleep, sir. This is a large house."

Hank ducked into his bedroom. He reappeared in the hallway moments later wearing jean pants, a suit jacket. He shuffled through his car key drawer until he was happy with his selection and went to go out the door.

"Right. Well I'm off to get a dog or two."

"Shall I call Mr. Hammer and get a security sweep?"

"Yeah. Find a Basquiat to buy, upgrade the system. Tell him it's for the art. Whatever the fuck."

And with that Hank slammed his door and scanned the bushes around the house. The sun was high and the day was bright. There was nowhere to hide. His was the only house for thirty acres. Satisfied that no one was watching he got into his car and drove off.

10.

Late morning and Marcus was flopping around in his bed, wondering why his cock was always hard in the morning. His dreams weren't always provocative, still he'd wake up and be hard as onix. What the fuck. The birds bid him a good day, sweat still thick on his sheets. Air conditioning unit stuck in the window, tho not working. It's a wonder he ever got any sleep at all. Especially after what happened the previous night.

Hitch and them had gotten back to Argon, on a whim. Just as they swarmed a call rang through his head. They'd fitted him with an earpiece, could hear most things emergency responders were doing. 'Almost like Superman?' he'd remembered asking. 'Almost,' Hitch had said. The breeze begged for something to happen, the trees around Argon pined for it as well. There was police jargon Marcus did not understand. Once the call came through Hitch looked at him, begging the kid with his eyes, even through the mask 'it's up there, play it cool. Show us what you're built with.

The streetlights were never on, so certainly they were not last night. Shouting, shouting was the only thing heard, 'You motherfucker!' it sounded like it was in the middle of everything. Marcus, Hitch, and company surrounding like white wolves. There was a silent knowledge amongst them. Some silent, in-sync, voice begged them to do what the rest of mankind could not. Listen. React on what makes the most sense. Marcus felt it all well up in him, hearing chords pop out in the conifers. 'You know it used to only be you black motherfuckers who would say motherfucker!' Someone shouted.

They reached the middle of the street. Lights started turning on inside homes, people stirred. A uniformed officer had a man in a headlock, gun drawn, asking for a reason to shoot. 'Don't you struggle,' he'd whispered.

Hitch spoke, the officer quaked in his little shitty pants, he'd not seen any of them approach. "What'd he do, officer?" Hitch was cool, collect. Marcus vibrated along with the strings controlling everything, vying a chance at becoming a part of the universe himself, to see how it would all go.

"This little fucking punk didn't stop when I told him to."

Hitch sighed, "what was he doing before that?"

"Crossing the street, fits a description of some guy who killed that kid last night."

"Fits the description? Hardly seems like a good reason for a gun to his head." The group stood around, light finding way to their eyes.

"Look, Hitch, a kid died last night. Don't get all social justice on me. Where the fuck were you? I'm just doing what I can. He's got the tattoo, not just because he's black."

"Then why are you taunting him, motherfucker? Lotsa niggas with tattoos around here," Emcee spoke up. THe n-word sounded weird over a voice modulator.

"Who are you?"

"Your mother, bitch." Marcus was going to go on, enraged. Waiting for this cop to call to him a 'boy,' but then, he saw the face of the man with the gun to his head. It was one of the assholes who'd tried to jump Theo earlier, the guy driving. He gave Hitch a glance, Hitch knew, 'he's not innocent.' It was fucking incredible, Hitch made for that asshole even before Marcus had, tho not in time. He'd pulled a knife from somewhere and stabbed the cop in the neck. What a terrible sound, blood, gurgling, death. Marcus had trounced the guy only seconds after, Salem was in the police cruiser and pulled around. He and Rye stuffed the cop in and sped off, gone.

More cop cars could be heard in the distance, no doubt making a bee-line toward Argon. The cops assailant struggled under Emcee until Hitch kicked him in the head and hog-tied him, telling Marcus to go home before the entire neighborhood came out.

Marcus had went to bed right then, exhausted. And now he was awake on a brand new day.

He turned on the news to find that the story was already out. A cop had been stabbed and a man had been arrested. The police officer had lived thanks to a good Samaritan driving him to the hospital. No mention of Marcus' shadow warriors ever came about. The news proclaimed they had an interview with the woman who drove the officer to the hospital. Marcus laughed because he never realized how much shit the news made up until this point. The big titted woman whom was half in tears on his television was definitely not the one who got the officer to the hospital.

Marcus watched the television for a few more minutes to see if there was anything about his new team. Nada. Zilch. Zero. Nill. None. Love.

Knock Knock

Marcus got up and answered the door. Zee stood in front of him, looking angry and defeated.

"Bruh." Zee managed to say, eyes on Marcus' porch. Zee was a rather large guy. He was tall, and had a good mix of muscle and fat. His body frame was wide and hard to hold up, though Zee always managed to do so happily. Now, he gave no effort to hold upright. "I need your help man."

56

Marcus gave Zee another once over, slumped against his door. "Come on."

Zee slithered passed Marcus and frumped down on his couch. Marcus tapped a few buttons on his stereo as a heavy bass thumped a hole into his speakers. He sat down next to Zee and broke open a cigarillo, emptying its contents. Tobacco was replaced with ground up marijuana. A little fancy thumb work granted it all to be rolled up, superfluously. Marcus held one end and burned the other.

He wouldn't ask Zee what was up. That question would hang around until it asked itself. Zee looked into his hand until Marcus handed him the funky pencil. Zee took two slow hits, leaned back, and exhaled. "You know George Hammer?" He asked.

Marcus took a second, remembering, smiling at the irony of just having met the guy. "Yeah," he said, simply.

"I fucked up man."

"How?"

"Well, when we were first starting out we needed all that equipment and then the dude was just a phone call away if we wanted some girls or some drugs. I figured, you know, that you would blow up and start bringing in the money. How much we owed the guy wouldn't matter."

Marcus sat wordless as Zee went into how it all happened. George'd lend money out to people with some interest. He'd break a kneecap here or a few ribs there if he wasn't paid back. Zee had a broken leg awhile back but had just told Marcus it was from falling or some dumb shit.

Zee had needed money for a studio when they realized what Marcus could do on a microphone. Every second Marcus wasn't making songs was another second wasted. Zee did what he had to get the equipment needed. He had even paid back George in a timely manner on everything from the switchboard to the synthesizer to the metronome. But with that came the bottles in the VIP section, the narcotics, and the strippers. Zee never wanted to be a producer who couldn't make it rain on a stripper.

The blunt was half out before Marcus spoke up again.

"How bad is it?"

"He wants me to stage a heist on one of those jewelers he's running security for." Zee said, using air quotes around the word 'security'. "I owe him too much, bro. It's the only way I can pay him back."

Marcus sat and thought about the irony. He wasn't flashy. He had no gold chain or twenty thousand dollar watch. If he had to get into town he'd catch a ride with someone or just walk. The most expensive thing he owned was his microphone. Then he realized the most expensive thing he had was probably his affinity for grass and bitches. Now it was catching up to him. Zee always said not to worry about it so Marcus never did. He just assumed his music really was making all that money. But all the shows he'd done had been free. Even most of his mixtapes were just handed out to whomever would have them. Marcus had fans he'd never seen or heard of before. Fans are priceless. Eventually they'd pay to support him but for now they hadn't so much as afforded him a roll of asshole saving toilet paper. He'd like to blame Zee entirely, but could not.

"Will you help me?" Zee asked.

"Yeah, but once this is over we're done not being frugal."

"Scouts honor. I will be one niggardly nigger." Zee smiled. Tension seemed to rise off him as some unknown force lifted boulders off his back. He sat up and hit the blunt one last time, "we gotta do it tomorrow night. He has a scheduled security shutdown and reboot that will last about three minutes. We gotta be in and out."

"Tomorrow night?" Marcus asked.

"Yeah, is that alright with you?"

"No, yeah, I just. Do we have to do it at night?"

"What? Are you afraid of those big bad Dark Defenders? Man what do those Robin Hood lookin' dudes know about a mac-eleven?"

"No, no, it's good we just have a show tomorrow night."

"No we don't. We're doing this."

Marcus decided to change the subject. If Zee didn't forget about this whole thing than at least Marcus wouldn't have to talk to him about it right now. He had to figure out how this would work out, Emcee-wise. He got Zee rambling about some musical nonsense. Something about a saxophone and two thirds timing.

Sidebar: The guy who played saxophone in Zee's beats was High G. High G was High G's favorite note and anytime someone asked how he was doing he'd respond "I'm high, G". Sometimes he'd refer to himself as "a high G" or "the high G".

Once Zee got going on thinking about music a trip to his lab would soon follow. He had to get to work. Saxophones turned into trumpets and before long Zee had a full song floating around in his head. It would float away if he didn't put it down.

Almost on cue Zee got up, chucked a peace sign, and left Marcus with this. "The dude sets it up so we can make a clean getaway. What could go wrong?"

Yeah, Marcus, what could go wrong?

11.

"Rise and shine, porcupine" Ben pounded on a shed door. A groan came from within and soon Hector came out, holding a dufflebag. "Late night?"

"Yeah."

"When are you going to tell them about Monica?"

"Look, I don't want to talk about this right now. I gotta get to work. Hitch will fucking flip, too, if he comes out right now."

Hector brushed by Ben and sauntered off.

He's going to get us killed, Ben thought as he stared at the mess of curly red hair that was Hector Bridge. Ben had known about Hec and Monica's love affair before they had. She had laughed once--this was over a year ago--at a joke he'd made and then caught Hec's eye just a little too long, like she was sizing up his soul to see if they may be compatible. Ever since then Hec was the first person to address her. The others hadn't noticed because they were big dumb emotional idiots who just thought Hec was doing his job. You know, Birdie talks to Monica, Hitch talks to George, and Rye talks to Asher.

He was worried about how much Monica might know due to excess pillow talk. Hector might not have divulged anything, but people do the stupidest shit when they are in love.

Hitch's zany rules had kept them safe, but really no one had come for them. The cops once, one guy went on TV and said he had their identities, 'tune in at 9!' but the big reveal was less than fruitful. The whistleblower had no whistle to blow, fucking idiot couldn't even make the sound with his mouth. He'd called out four random people who had alibis for everything. When he was questioned later he admitted to, 'shooting in the dark, playing random numbers on the lottery,' just hoping he was right. "I flipped through the phone book and picked four random people," he squealed, foot in his ass, tears on his face, "I just wanted people to like me."

People see things and then proceed forget them all the time. Faces, voices, actions, sounds. If someone saw Salem running in uniform, he kept going. Salem'd just be a story told to a few friends. If he'd been lucky enough to be seen by a pothead, the whole incident will have been forgotten about almost instantaneously.

"Hey." Hitch called from up on his porch, locking it and bringing two bikes down. "Take the long way. I'll see you there."

Ben got onto his and pedaled off.

Soon Ben met a large-steel-blue-door, unlocking it, drawing it up. Inside was a storage facility turned shop. Dark dirt bikes stood lifted in the air and were surrounded by tools, parts. Hitch was off in a corner, already at work.

They thought nothing of their phones buzzing back at Hitch's. Hank was calling the two fervently but to no avail. Ben and Hitch were twisting springy wickets and lubing up some rims. Ben kicked the music to a deafening roar over the already whirring power tools.

Each bike were special ordered by Hank to each fit its mounter suitably. Marcus' stood in all black with a dark grey trim. The black paint had a matte finish, almost like the bike itself would absorb any trace of light and soak it to the core. The sprockets were black. The rims were black. If death had a dirt bike, you could bet this would be it.

Each of the bikes were mainly black and came equipped with a grappling hook between the handlebars. A nitrous tank sat next to the back wheel and they were each, somehow, silent as the wind.

Hitch and Ben were fervently caught in their tune-ups, and the music was loud.

KNOCK KNOCK

Hitch cut the music out and went to open the large, garage-like, door. The sound of dogs barking slammed harshly against the cement walls of the unit. Hank stood grinning with three snarling mongrels leashed in his hands. The brightness from the sun flowed in and caused Ben temporary blindness. Hank stepped in and brought his mutts with him.

"'Sup nerds. I see you aren't answering those fancy satellite phones I bought you."

"Shut up. I'll set your nitrous to blow. Trust fund dickwad." Ben replied.

Hank brought his dogs forward and introduced them. "Yeah, well, say hello to Skip, Fred, and Jose."

"Do they double as male strippers?"

"Har-har-har. Some sicko broke and entered my house the other night. He won't be leaving with his testicles if he decides to come again."

"Can you say that last part again?"

"If he decides to come again." Rye said, looking confused for a second then realization dawned on him. "Fuck off," he said, grin on his face.

"Someone broke into your house?" Hitch finished up a gas tank refill.

Hank went through his story and showed the video to his companions. Ben was more disturbed than was Hank which disturbed Ben even more. If this, whoever he was, decided to come back he would be put on full notice as to why no one fucked with Hank. Still, Ben felt uneasy. He'd say this man seemed sure of himself but that wouldn't quite be right. He seemed like he already knew what this evidence would bring, especially because it was delivered right to Hank's door.

"All right, Hank, stay in tonight. We'll be fine with Marcus. Keep an eye on your place. Let us know if anything goes bump in the night. We'll be there."

"Oh, he'll be on the floor long before you get there."

"I know. It looks like he's alone but he may not be."

"Right, c'mon boys," Hank said to his dogs, hopping into his SUV.

In the time it would take Hank to arrive back at his château Hitch and Ben were done. The both of them grabbed a bite, separately, and retired.

So, Ben got back to his story, shoes off, pants off in the corner, beer in hand. His current bit of entertaining nonsense had pitted good against evil--I know, I know, a paradigm shifting idea--in one of Ben's favorite settings, France in the early 1940's. If the Nazi's weren't enough, the monsters on the French countryside surely would be. This story was more or less for fun as a majority of it would be depictions of anti-Semites being ripped apart limb by limb. Ironically, his monsters were the good in this story, helping rid the world of a true underworldly scourge. Ben couldn't really solve the problems of man, but he could surely use his imagination to dish out punishment. Not that a jew or two didn't also get eaten. Demon spawns don't really discriminate, when it comes down to it.

The click click click of his typing numbed Ben's mind into oblivion, portraits wound and begged to be on the page; it was not enough. Never would be. *We make great jesters*, he led in,

64

fools in the foxhole. If I'm being truthful I don't like 'um that much either. But to go s'far as shelling the 166th to defend a tiny angry guy with a murdering problem, I think not. Smokes in hand, Johnny-whatshisname-on my left.   Laughing, 'these stupid sonsabitches,' on my mind.   Once we took Normandy the war was over....

12.

Basketball: Hector, Theo bonded. Elsewhere gangbangers were probably exchanging crack with a shaky hobo but for now Theo was beating Hector, 10-8. Hector had size but Theo had skill. It was hard for Hector to keep track of a mini-man who flashed lightning crossing over. Not to mention the kid had an uncanny ability to twist himself around, help the ball avoid Hec's outstretched hand.

Hector checked the ball up to Theo and he slashed to the left before slamming the ball against the ground behind Hector's back, spinning around the large ginger, the ball met him on the other side of Hector's body. He chucked his head towards the basket, Hector hesitated, and Theo had an easy basket before anyone could say boomshakalaka.

The day was bright, breezy, and the hornets' nest behind the backboard had been disposed of. The asphalted court was just warm enough to help rubber soles grip and shift directions. The rim was single, as Hector had lodged many complaints to get rid of the double rims the net used to dangle from. The sound of laughter, birds, and dribbling flooded Hector's senses as his mind clarified how beautiful this moment would be remembered. The air was thick with the things that made Hector want to staredown treelines and remember each passing second with a fond nostalgia.

Hector went to get his check from Theo who looked at him with quiet confusion.

"Are we not playing to 11?" Theo asked, clearly reveling in his victory.

"Yeah, no, give me a second to breathe. We'll go one more."

"So why isn't Marge here today?"

"Oh she-a, she, decided to pursue other dreams of hers."

"Really? 'Cus Greg told me him and Heather walked into her office and she had one of those giant black dildos halfway up her hoochie."

Heather was next to be in charge, Greg was her little brother; Marge had a bit of a masturbation problem. When Hector first witnessed what he could only describe as a whale with the libido of a thirteen year old boy, he had to choke down what he could only describe as vomit. He swore to not tell and he wouldn't. Something like that was only meant to be forgotten.

Unfortunately--or perhaps in timely auspicion--Heather found out Marge, and she was released. She packed up all her binders, plaques, thank you letters, staples, pens, pencils, dildos, tape, sticky notes, KY, plugs, earplugs, and so forth; placed them in her car with the entire community center watching. She came there every day. Every. Day. And now she would come there no longer.

Hector did not want to be caught in this conversation. "Well, some people have problems."

"Yeah well that's still fucked up. I mean what if I were to walk in on that? I don't need to see any dildo play at my fragile age."

"Yeah, I know. What'd your mom make for breakfast this morning?"

"Oh, she didn't come home. Probably just had to stay over a few hours. Justine made me pancakes."

Hector felt his taste buds cringe. It wasn't every day that Christine stayed at her apartment instead of going home, but it happened often enough. Justine was a notorious pancake maker. Hector did not like her very much.

"Hey, Hec, you ever eat pancakes and after a while you just think about how you wish you were eating anything else?" Theo inquired, tossing Hector the ball.

"I don't eat pancakes." Hector replied.

"I'm about at that point. Yeah, maybe I'll stop eating pancakes too."

"Best decision I ever made."

The two played one on one until they developed a fair amount of blisters. Theo had won out the day, taking four games of seven. Hector had half a joke in his mind: a superhero losing to a kid in basketball. There was something there only not enough. Hector stunk, but at least he didn't just get fired for masterbating too much. They all gathered in preparation for their final meeting of the day, now led by the lovely, and newly in-charge, Heather Raulston. Raulston's tits were the type that could even shake and jump in a t-shirt; nothing seemed to be able to confine them. There was a sweetness in her walk and whenever she smiled she appeared to be fighting off the urge to also be aroused. Her brunette hair usually hung carefree, twirling at the ends. Today it did the same. Finding a shirt her tits *didn't* look great in was a known impossible task, boyo did they look good in today's low-cut number.

And you should see her ass.

Heather was practically shaking from excitement, on stage, as she discussed future plans and wished everyone a good weekend. Hector watched as every eyeball in the room looked directly at her shaking bosoms, Gay Randy included. They were all thinking the same thing.

Do you think she'll masterbate in her office, too?

Heather attempted to dodge the kids' questions about why Marge had left, and these kids were quick, eventually they were all laughing and chanting 'Large Marge! Large Marge!', all the kids around Hector asking him if Large Marge were a sex freak. Yes, technically she was, but he looked at each child like they'd asked if the sky were purple and rained doodoo.

After the meeting was over they were all free to go. Hector went to his locker to grab his shit; Heather came strolling over to meet him.

"Hey, you wanna go grab a drink later? I gotta go home and shower and get ready but you wanna meet at Hund's, around seven?" She asked.

"Does a cookie crumble?"

"What?"

"Are pigs bacon? Does Jesus save? Did I not shoot the deputy, but the sheriff?" Hector was really trying to get that arousal laced smile to break on Heather's lips. It did. The smile was enough of a 'see you there' as Hector needed. He closed his locker, smiled back, and went to go find Theo.

Theo was leaning outside against bricks, stacked up, brick and mortar made great walls for the community center. Young minds and their role models were next to him standing or squatting while they wrestled with their bicycle locks. The sun hit the bricks on the side of the building enough to make them warm. Theo soaked in this warmth as he scoped out the activity around him; the coolness with which he did this should not go unnoted, Hector had always been a little green over how Theo seemed to permeate everything around him and not be changed by it.

A whistle or two sounded, Hec looked over his shoulder to see Heather leaving the building. Wowee. A few *oh yeah's* and another whistle followed. The late afternoon light bounced off of her body and somehow made it more curvy, tho not vivacious, far more reserved tho still confident in all she had-- so to speak--working for her. Hector fought off the erection that was starting to take form, imagining his blood flowing back up into his arms. It drove him mad, they all did; with words or perhaps something quite different they all would, eventually. His stare lasted long enough for Theo to creep up, unnoticed.

"Damn, look at that white bitch. Look at those hips. Does that ass come with its own zip code? Are those her nipples? You think Jesus had women like that throwing themselves at him? Damn, that nigga musta been gay."

Hector broke out of his trance and cracked a smile at Theo. "Why do you think all of his disciples were men?"

"Damn, Hec. Blasphemous heathen doesn't even begin to describe what kind of fucked up you are." Theo turned to make his way towards State so that he could make his way towards Argon. Hector broke into a brisk walk, catching up.

"I work with kids all day. I do good. If that feckless douche doesn't want to let me in to his cloud filled house because of a joke than he can suck my cock."

"Dude."

"Fear not young Theo. The big man has a sense of humor. I'd like to think he finds most of his yucks in irony."

"Aaron Sorkin ass...." Theo stopped walking and looked down at the ground. His eyes focused in on nothing at all. It was clear that most of his sight was shifted thoughtfully inward. "You mean like when a kid gets shot for selling baking soda?"

"I hope not." Hector responded.

The two walked in relative silence all the way back to Theo's house. The air was thick with some serious conversation that Hector could not force himself to get into. The silence between them seemed to give more solace than any conversation could. What words would make Theo feel better about inadvertently getting his friend shot? Hector threw around ideas of it being the fault of Theo's maker but he knew it would be bullshit. So, he reverted to asking Theo questions regarding the weather or the baseball. Theo hated baseball, and small talk. Truth be told Hector was no fan of small talk either.

As they approached Theo's porch-steps a cloud still hung weightily around them.

"I know it's not my fault." Theo said, the lie didn't make him feel any better at his core. But it was enough to ease his mind. "I didn't pull the trigger. If I would've known I'd never've done   it."

"I know, Thee, I know. We all make decisions we come to regret." Hector said. "Tell your mom I say hello. I'll see you tomorrow. You going to keep coming to the community center when school lets out?"

"Probably. Summer gets pretty crazy around here."

"Right." Hector said. And he hugged the little dude. He wasn't sure why. Theo was a strong kid. In that brief moment when Theo was resting against him Hector wanted to disclose everything. Nothing would harm Theo, not on Birdie's watch. Theo disengaged and allowed a smile to flicker across his face, though he was looking at the ground so Hector would not see.

"And I thought Jesus was gay." Theo said, looking back up at Hector. He tried to rid his face of the grin that adorned it but could not.

With a final goodbye Theo retreated into his house. Hector descended from the porch and began his walk up to State and over home. Soon he would be meeting Heather Raulston for a drink.

Hund's was a nifty little piece of architecture. It was a two story bar with a patio out behind it. It would have been run down to sober eyes but those of the inebriated variety found it quaint. Dollar bills hung from every inch of the ceiling like green, anecdote covered, icicles. The walls were a multitude with classic album covers, license plates, and other tokens of appreciation that seemed to be thrown up almost randomly, more than likely to cover up holes in the wall. The upstairs was less flattering as it looked more like the metaphorical hole in the wall. The patio was where the real charm kicked in as strands of lights hung from every which way to give the warm evenings that dream-like feeling drunks everywhere longed for.

Hector was almost on State when he heard footsteps pounding on the street behind him. He was vaguely aware of Theo screaming his name. He sounded so wounded that Hector's mind almost tuned him out completely, fearful that the screams might resurrect its own traumas. Nevertheless, the screams persisted behind a buzzing and screeching which pounded in his ears. *HEC!!*

Buzz buzz buzz

HEC!!!

Buzz buzz buzz.

Hector began to feel like a wandering ghost, he began to look like one too. The color left his face; the heat, his body. His stomach sank as his entire body began to panic. Breathing seemed to be a forgotten and lost art. He felt his knees tremble, the point of no return was nigh. He was grasping for sanity with hands that had no thumbs when he remembered that what was going on was entirely due to his lack of oxygen. He forced his diaphragm up and then down.

"HEC!!!!!!" Theo's voice sounded not so distant, in fact it was nearly directly behind Hector. He turned and found Theo still running and screaming down Argon, waving what appeared to be a small piece of paper in the air. His screams brought the porch dwellers out to the edge of the street. His face was panic, his feet could barely keep the pace his body wanted to go. This overexertion caused a violent and painful tumble. Hector was running back down Argon before Theo hit the pavement, his body grunging with a thump halfway between his house and where Hector had previously been standing. Theo rolled around on the pavement, half writhing, cursing as many gods as he could think of.

Hector didn't want to know what could cause such distress. He wanted to run. Wanted to see Theo tomorrow at the center and realize that this was all some scenario his fucked up mind had hallucinated. Theo managed to get on all fours just to pound his fist into the warm asphalt. The piece of paper he had been waving around lay a few feet from where he now tried to put a hole in the earth. Hector faltered as he half stumbled his way over to what he now recognized as the back of a picture.

"What could be this bad?" Hector found himself saying out loud.

His fingers trembled; he decided not to turn over the picture. Instead he went back to Theo and grasped him the way a bouncer might a drunk; he was a human straight jacket. Theo wriggled but quickly gave in, limping his body while his energy focused up on his tear ducts.

"Fuck fuck fuck," The kid mumbled to himself.

Theo withdrew when he was let go. He turned around and forced his ducts to swallow down what was left.

People say that the eyes don't lie but they can. When the brain doesn't know to respond it freezes until it comes to a sensible solution, often times this semi-second of a hesitation is enough evidence to people who seek out lies; whatever comes out of the hesitator's mouth is a lie. Hector hoped that Theo's eyes were lying when they faced him and only expressed terror, enough terror to work gooseflesh in to Hector's lungs, forcing his breathe to hinder in strength. No, Hector was sure that what he had seen in Theo's eyes was nothing but an over-exaggeration of what was inked on the picture not four feet from where Hector grasped a child, who sounded so broken that Hector would have given his soul to play the mender. Perhaps, at that very moment, his subconscious had inked a deal with something which only meant to destroy him. Almost instantly Theo came to. Hector reached for the photo.

"Don't." Theo said, the hurt in his soul could be heard in the word. "If the wind blows strong enough it may just go away." His eyes didn't waver from the nothingness they were focused on.

The suddenness of Hector's next thought shot through him, why hadn't he contemplated Christine's absence from this little rendezvous before now? She was always around when Hector dropped off young Theo. Surely if she was anywhere in the vicinity of her screaming off-spring she would come running, motherly arms outstretched and itching to console. This was the moment Hector's mind would reference once he had seen the picture; his hindsight had already made note of this very moment, and would cite it when he realized later on that he knew who was on the picture, even before he saw it.

Uneasily, Hector grasped the photograph and turned it over. The first thing he saw was her head. It was displayed

74

prominently in the center of a slanted, wooden-roofed, room which could not be mistaken for anything but an attic. An attic with a rather large amount of junk and a rather small amount of space. What the room looked like hadn't really sunk in for Hector, he was sucked in to the sight of Christine's head, laying sideways on the floor in a small piddle of blood. The smooth ebony of her lifeless eyes buried themselves into Hector's, now almost as lifeless, baby blues.

Theo tried to take it away from Hector at this point, perhaps Hector should have allowed it. "Stop man, you'll go insane."

The attic was the one above the community center. A window hung, half-boarded, behind Christine's head, outside of this window was a basketball court whose only two occupants wore the same blue and yellow shirts Hector and Theo currently adorned. This was no trick. That was definitely the two of them playing basketball not two hours ago. Hector went through all the *what the fucks* in his mind but could not come up with a sensible amount of anything. Christine's head lay motionless and blood soaked. Christine, who had just whispered much a sweet nothing into his ear not twelve hours ago. *But where is*…Hector spotted one of her arms on top of a box in the corner, and then her torso; which was completely behind another box, but could be seen by way of a mirror.

"It's a game or some shit," Theo said, once again staring to the distance, "like I Spy or Where's Waldo."

It was all a fucking joke. The whole thing. The picture was taken a mere 50 feet from where the two were playing basketball, the angle making a mockery of the day-dreaming Hector below. Hector found her ear after the torso and couldn't play along for another second, fear of losing one's sanity is never a good time. As soon as he looked away an unsurmountable anger rose up from somewhere deep in his belly, out of the vault his trapeze artist had forgotten about, he became even more angered by his own anger, and around that carousel went until he vomited everywhere.

Hector collected himself as best he could and sat next to Theo; his head hung between his knees.

"Why would it be important that both of us saw?"

"What?"

"I mean I know I may have made enemies the other day but nobody this fucking depraved. What aren't you telling me, Hec?" Theo asked both questions with his head still between his legs. "And why did you look so hurt when you saw? You barely ever said two words to my moms. Sometimes you throw her the usual nice-white-guy-greeting but damn. I don't know man this thing's got me fucked up."

"Me too." Hector responded. Suddenly he remembered something that was peculiar enough to be overlooked, a phantom in the corner of his eye.

His mind went reeling to last night, and his ill-guided descent onto Christine's porch. Fuck, Christine. Hector hurled through the sky and created his own breeze to set his sail, descending to a woman who was as kind as she was brown and supple. The night was cool and the adrenaline was a-flowin'. Then his peripheral caught a darkness that could not be ignored. He shifted his focus, tilted his head just enough to see the room behind Christine's patio, inside of her apartment, and the phantom he was chasing had disappeared. Hector chalked it up to light tricks but his subconscious would not. It was positive it saw gangly, animalistic, hair somewhere in the blur.

13.

Ben had just enough time to crap out a few pages before he had to be out for the night. The video Rye had shown him reminded Ben of a darker time, one where he had watched his father die without even knowing it. This was nothing new, his Fantastic Fucktards were frequent receivers of hate mail, but the eyes of the man who broke and entered Rye's fortress were blacker than the eyes of the man who killed his father, leaving Ben terrified of what may come next.

Ben spent the next few hours in front of his typer, ticking away a story he should have left lie, but could not.

I suppose we should start with John. He was a friend to all of my friends, and was also a friend of mine. He was a little off his rocker, he'd grown tough with a father who liked drugs and lying more than he liked anything or anyone: whose narcissism flirted heavily with every kind of sociopathic tendency.

One day we were told to believe John had plotted to kill his brother, Dale. When we reheard the same story the next day Dale told us it was actually the father who'd been plotted against. Then the next time we'd heard the story Dale was back to telling us it was him, not his father. Even some straight stories don't make sense, how was this one supposed to hold up?

Word was he had written letters to a friend, about how he'd like to kill his father--or his brother, depending on which version. The twelve stand up citizens who heard the case believed whatever story was told to them over the course of the hearing. John's father sobbed on the bench as he described his son, so mentally incapable, sick, that he'd plotted to kill the man who'd given him life.

Now might be a good time to let all you good folks know that John was never the type to hurt someone, he was an easy scapegoat, and how he'd been raised had caused quite a few eyebrows to be lifted by the good people who were in charge of psychology at his high school.

On the day in question--when John was supposedly supposed to kill his father--the cops had been "tipped off" that John had weapons on him, weapons he would use to kill. So they searched John as he walked home from school, found the hammer and pack of nails and figured that was reason enough to send him to a mental institution.

While there we, being myself and John's other friend Steve, were told he had hallucinations of spiders in his ears and would masterbate onto girls while in the lunch line.

John was very private about his masturbation habits, it was well documented.

He was out after one year and back in after three months; his therapist, whom his father paid, had said he was not fit for society, that he may hurt himself or others if not constantly monitored.

After another considerable stay amongst the unwell John came back different, convinced he was as bad as he was told he was.

His father, Brock, and girlfriend Tibby decided this was a good time to let John out on his own, fresh off the nuthouse, on his eighteenth birthday. They kicked him out. It didn't make sense.

I still remember the last time I saw John. We were playing basketball over at the park, three on three with a few subs, and his eyes still glowed like John's had, full of life. That was the day he told us his parents had sent him walking off the plank. He found an apartment and a job, but he would be almost an hour away.

Three weeks later he was dead, overdose, we were told. His father had found him, lying like a fish in a waterless bathtub. Oddly enough his father was alone, his was the only story to go off.

He had wandered in to John's apartment one day, just a normal check-in, and had found the place all tidied up. Normally John was not tidy tho not untidy either, however even the slightest mess or run away dust bunny warranted a good berating from old Brock Opti. Anyway, the place was spotless when Brock walked in and decided to walk around, said he figured John wasn't home but he still wanted to check for "drugs," 'he had a drug problem,' Brock said on the stand. 'I had to keep a close eye.' I'd never seen John do anything but smoke a little pot.

He went into the bathroom and found John's body staring at him from the tub, overdosed on cocaine. Brock said there was a bag of it in the bedroom but the police had noticed the bag was unopened and there was little to no cocaine residue anywhere besides in John's stomach, of which there was so much it had hardened into a softball shaped rock.

Two days later there was no burial, just a cremation and ashes thrown over a bridge.

He was off his meds, they said.

He had developed a heavy drug addiction over the course of three weeks, they said.

He successfully attempted at suicide, they said

He was sick, they said

Myself and Randy, John's other friend, didn't quite believe it. It was possible, sure, but there was a skunk in the henhouse, stinking up the place. John's father, a man who thought everyone wanted to out him anyway, became very aware of our mistrust in his story.

"Ben," he'd say to me "get out of my doorway."

I had gone over there every week since John's passing and knocked on his door till he answered. Questioned every detail. One day I guess I pushed a little too hard.

I remember walking up to his door for the tenth or so time and knocking. I was alone this time, usually Randy was with me. Brock opened the door in his usual semi-friendly manner and I said hello.

"Where's your boyfriend?" Brock asked, the stink of whiskey and cocaine-sweat thick on his body.

"Did he leave a note?"

"Well, yes, but only I saw it. I burned it with his body, it hurt too much."

"What'd it say?"

"Oh that this was the final 'fuck you' to his poor father. I had given him a life not worth living. And now he decided the best way to get back at his old man was to clean his place the way he knew I liked, eat a softball of cocaine, and die in the tub. For how am I to live with killing my son?"

"How are you supposed to live with it?" I asked. His eyes locked on mine and he knew I was not speaking metaphorically. A few things flashed through his face in that instant: fear, anger, fear again, embarrassment, loathing, and then nothing. His gaze had drawn blank, the awful man he was finally coming to the surface, and he cracked a smile.

"Get on out of here before you end up with him. Why, I could make yours look like a choke-n-stroke. For shame Ben, masturbating so much that it killed you, for shame."

I ran as he stood there cackling like the lunatic he was, bent over, belly aching, singing wretched things in to the evening. I had to go tell Randy. Randy was coaching youth basketball at the elementary school by the graveyard.

Well, the sun was setting as my run came to a brisk walk not a mile from the elementary school. I caught my wind and ran the rest of the way. I entered the building in a huff, paid the two dollar entrance fee, and sat on the edge of the bleacher seats, catching my wind once more. The game was nearly over but it could not end soon enough. I had to tell Randy so we could come up with some kind of plan.

As I sat I could see out the gym doors and into the lobby. I saw him walk in through the front door and unload a clip at random, hitting trophy cases as well as people. After his initial barrage the world went mad. Screams were the first sound to slice through the air. Then it was crying, then it was the thunderous parade of elephants that meant fans descending from bleachers. Mothers grabbed their sons, 911 was dialed, and I just sat there looking at this man who was only staring at me while reloading whatever pistol he had.

"On second thought," he yelled over the hysteria, "maybe I'll just kill you now!"

A man tried to run by Brock for the door but was cut off by a bullet to his leg.

I almost didn't see Randy until the last second, a blur that had come seemingly out of nowhere to tackle Brock to the ground. I truly thought Randy had caught him by surprise, he was moving that quickly. But with a move as skilled as it was heartless Brock took the smooth carbon fiber of his gun and pulled the trigger as soon as the muzzle found its way into Randy's oncoming mouth.

Once Randy was dead Brock began to make his way towards me. I was still seated, bewildered at what my eyes were seeing.

"Hey kid!" I heard someone call. I turned my head to see a man in dark uniform. "You may want to move, that guy has a gun."

81

What an asshole *I thought. I knew the uniform he wore well, mainly from the news, gossip. In our town there have been, for quite some time, glorified night watchmen parading around the night like vigilantes. Beating on muggers, saving cats from trees, fixing stop signs. Once the grandeur of having heroes in our town wore off, they were really an afterthought to the law-abiding locals.*

One more of these masked men came out of the double doors adjacent of the bleachers. I looked out of the gymnasium and saw another sprinting down the steps right off of the elementary school's lobby.

"Ben!" One more screamed at me from atop the bleachers, I hadn't even seen him enter. I stood and faced him. "Get the fuck out of here!" The man called.

His figure was familiar but I could not put my finger on where from. Had he been close enough for me to see his eyeballs I would have known right away. His voice was muffled by the screams but it had sounded…

BANG

Another shot rang out as the air beside my ear was replaced by with a bullet. Brock had closed the gap between us, and fast. The man who stood above me raced down the seats to get to me with desperation. Brock was reloading and just coming through the gymnasium doors when my hero jumped at him from ten rows above the floor. Again, Brock's reflexes had proven to best a cat's and he caught the man in mid air, above his head, and used momentum to propel him into the wall.

The other two vigilantes who were in the gym hurried towards crazy Brock Opti. The one who had been outside of the gym remained outside, just outside in fact, tending to the wounded with gauze, doing whatever he could.

Brock finished his reload and aimed his gun. The man sat slumped on the floor, woozy from slamming into the wall.

Something in the way he tried to get up shouted familiarity and I knew before I knew that this man's life was important to me.

Brock's back turned, hulking and stone hard, I decided to make my attack.

I hit his back, my legs thrust forward with as much force as my adrenaline would allow, but soon felt the urge to crumple. Brock had taken my full force attack and absorbed it with no problem, half of my attack had been pushed back into myself. He quickly spun and slammed his fist into the side of my head. The world spun and the colors began to pop in my ears. I felt his hand groping for my neck until he found it, picking me up and pinning me to the wall.

"WHAT IS TAKING YOU GUYS SO LONG!!!" I screamed. "TAKE THIS GUY DOWN!"

The moments I had just endured felt like enough time for the queen of England to rule for a full life and then die. In reality it had only taken a second or two, shocking the other masked men as much as it had myself.

The persona I had come to know as "Hitch" flashed out of the door he was waiting behind and slammed Brock square in his balls. Brock's grip loosened on my throat and I gave him my own swift kick to the baby maker. "Bird, go help Rye get those fucking people out of here." Hitch roared the orders and the other man he was with obliged, going out the double doors. The whining of ambulances was just outside.

Hitch quickly brought his fist up to Brock's jaw and he completely let go of my throat. I slumped, black in front of my eyes, I could hear inaudible groaning from the wall next to me. I reached for him but could not find him. I could tell he was reaching out to me, too, somehow. Slowly light again found my eyes.

Punch for punch, Hitch had fought off Brock and forced him to make distance from the two of us. I crouched down to help the man I must have known but the hero I did not. When I touched his

83

shoulder his eyes snapped open. So kind those eyes were, so protective, almost like…

"Ben." The man said. "Help me up."

I put my arm under his shoulder and helped the man to his feet. He requested that I slap him so I did. He smiled and said he was ready to go now. Hitch was having a hard time penetrating Brock's defenses and was ever wary of the gun that still waved in his hand.

I stood there for a moment and watched this man run into the fray, the reality of who he was slowly making its way into a thought I could know to be true. He threw himself at the man's waste just as Hitch had parried a blow and swung his foot low, relinquishing Brock's own feet from the floor. The two worked in beautiful cohesion. Brock's gun slid towards me as he hit the floor.

The knowledge my brain was slowly receiving was too awe inspiring for me to move. My fatheR, THAT'S who it was and he was subduing Brock with a skilled ease that made me well up with pride. I was locked there, watching the easy, steady, man I knew beat a murderer senseless. One punch, two punch, three punch, elbow. The speed and skill was something I should have known was within him but did not. Night shift my ass.

"Ben." A voice next to me said. Startled as I was I turned and instantly recognized the man who had seemingly appeared next to me. He was a friend of my father's. One who had come to the house before, Hank was his name, Rye was his persona. "You should really get out of here."

Just as he said this Brock had found strength within him and hurled my father off. Using his legs to make my father do a flip and land with a thud that many said caused the earthquake which rumbled through my small town at that very moment. Hitch, myself, and Hank all faltered and fell to the floor. It did not take us long to regain our balance but Brock was quicker, somehow. He had the gun in his hand in less than a flash and pointed it directly at my father.

"NOOOOOOOOOO" I screamed. Ran, begging. It was going to happen. And did. Brock took aim and barraged my father with the contents of his clip.

As soon as Brock was done firing Hitch subdued him with Rye quickly closing in as back-up.

Hitch tackled Brock to the floor and almost simultaneously Rye had swung his steel-toed boot directly to the man's head. Hitch punched the front of his face while Rye swung his foot at Brock's temple until his ears, nose, and mouth bled. By this time I was propped against the wall behind me, already wallowing in my grief.

Rye's kicks began to sound squishy, like he and Hitch were throwing blows at a fish. The blood of my father and my late friend's father pooled on the floor, no doubt ruining the finish on the wood grain. The sound of sirens flooded my ears as I noticed the shouts of paramedics' and mothers' and wives'. The loud disheartening shrills of fathers in pain also flooded the air. A man who was hurt enough to show the emotions I heard was a terrible thought. Hitch and Rye spat on the man as they vaulted out of the gymnasium's back doors, the cops came crashing through the front, where I sat.

"Fuck, they got here first." I heard one say.

"Jesus, is that Selby?" I heard another say.

"Kid, kid, KID!" One of the swine exclaimed. I could barely hear him but recognized that he must have been talking to me. I turned and met his face, tear ducts too shocked. "You alright?"

I stared blankly at him as my mind scrambled for an answer.

How many people must fall to the unjust? *My mind asked itself.*

85

It was at this very moment I decided to follow in my father's mask. I righted myself, without using the wall. Forced my feets one in front of the other as policemen looked at me like I was the most peculiar thing they had ever seen. I shuffled over to my father and pulled off his mask. In that brief moment where his mask was not yet off I convinced myself that I must have been wrong. This was some teacher I had forgotten about, a man I knew from work, or simply one who had been a fan of the heralding athleticism he had seen one Friday night when he decided to go see Greenmont High play a game of pigskin against the hated Yukon City Wreckers. It was not.

I was there holding his face. Pounding on the floor. Brock turned his face, now mangled, bloody, barely a face at all, and peeked at me through one of his eyes, sitting up. I sat back, waiting for my father to do the same. He did not. A terrible grin began to cross Brock's face; in his eyes I could see the police with their backs to us.

It was at this moment when I believed—for just an instant—that somebody out there was on my side. Maybe it was the universe righting some wrong it had bestowed upon me, or maybe it was just something that happens; the odds are always slim when they are stacked against you, but people still manage to win the lottery and get struck by lightning, and sometimes the man who deserved to die had a wad of blood-pumping veins in his head that would just not untangle.

"You little…shh…sh…sh…"

"Shit." I finished, watching Brock and semi-understanding that his brain was not doing so hot. He was suddenly incapable of meeting a gaze on anything. He still sat up but was convulsing. I watched him for a moment thinking maybe he had lost too much blood, or maybe that the pain from his jaw—which was unhinged and slagging as if a rubber band were holding it together—was too much for his weak mind to handle.

The thing about Brock is that he was a smoker, and the doctor said the type he liked were the only sticks on the market that were known to give folks aneurysms.

So by some miracle or happening or self-induced toxic build-up of brain fluid, Brock's ears started bleeding from the depths of his head, the very magma core of his being, and his mouth shot blood as if he were possessed.

You know, Omen style.

It took five seconds for the vessel burst to kill the man, though the doctor said that five seconds must have felt like an eternity. I'd like to think Einstein was correct in thinking time as relative, and an educated doctor man telling me that Brock had went through an eternity of mind-wrenching pain was enough for me to believe in hell.

"So do we not really die?" I asked the coroner a few hours later, surrounded by my father's kinfolk.

".....sure as hell looks dead to me." He responded, while scribbling notes onto his pad. "So he went insane, shot up a grade-school basketball game, and killed your father? Interesting," he asked and then said, looking thoughtfully into his white paper. "And then he got a brain aneurism. How very..."

"...mental." I replied.

"Had this happened twenty minutes earlier none of the following would have." He said to the four of us: myself, Hitch, Rye, and some quirky fellow called Birdie. "This monster be slain."

Ben removed himself from his typer and blew chunks out the window. Writing something like this made the memories all the worse. Not only did he have to remember them but he had to find the exact words to describe the nightmare in his mind, had to make it so real to himself that he could make it real to others. Usually writers take a liberty or

87

two when writing a story but this one lay as unembellished as his father lay dead in the ground.

Ben took a glance outside and realized night was well past its fast approach, the others were probably wondering where he was.

14.

Well, now, this interesting, thought Herald Overberger, sitting in his car. He was awaiting his girlfriend's arrival to the movie theatre.

Herald spotted a man sitting in the car parked rows back. There were a few other cars sprawled in to the night; the late show began twenty minutes prior. The parking lot swayed, not well lit, along it's curvature, only Herald and the car he'd saw spotted sat, idling.

Glancing in to his rearview, quickly, Herald saw the man, briefly but he was astute, aware. The top half of His body was painted completely in black. He had shoulder length hair that tangled and hung, or rather dangled, greasily around his face. The man's eyes were the first thing Herald noticed, their whiteness seemed to triple due to his black make-up. It was eerie how they seemed to glow. He looked away but thought the weirdo may have caught him somehow. Right, Herald shook the thought, only his interest tripled, he *had* to look again. He cursed himself, did so. The man was looking at a point, far off. Herald held his gaze, eventually fixating on the man's eyes, bleached white against his seemingly painted skin. They stared intently, Herald thought about the eyes themselves as their own living things, squirming in the eyes, having thoughts about what they saw. Herald spun and looked off where the man stared, just trees.

Where is she he thought, hoping the beautiful Heather Raulston hadn't stood him up. Thinking about Heather was only one quick step away from thinking about Heather's tits. Herald ran his hands through his thick red hair and sighed, the movie had started fifteen minutes ago and there hadn't been any activity in the parking lot for a half hour. Well, none except for...

...Herald glanced back in his mirror and the man was gone. Some primitive part of him began to panic. He felt like he was maybe the next victim in an old slasher film, the kind where that old slut bag Jenny sees someone in the bushes, but when she double-takes decides it was nothing, noticing wind rustling her shrubbery.

Knock Knock

Herald jumped in fright as he looked around for the origin of the knocks. He glanced from trunk to back door to passenger, seeing nothing and no one.

Maybe it was the wind he thought as he turned away from his passenger door.

He was so pre-occupied with looking everywhere else that he didn't notice the painted man standing right outside his own window. When he finally saw some odd flash of hair in the corner of his eye his scream came too late.

The man slammed his hand through Hector's window and grabbed the boy. His other hand grabbed a rather large piece of glass that had just shattered onto Herald's lap.

When the movie-goers were released from the theatre they found a boy lying on the blacktop, in his own blood, shards of glass randomly sticking out from his body: in the chest, legs, throat, one his eye, and a few stuffed into his mouth.

His driver's license and a note were pinned to one of the pieces in his leg. His name was circled on his license and the note read...

Whoops! This is not Hector. My apologies to the man in the wrong place at the wrong time. Herald, Hector, it's easy for an already confused man to mix up a syllable here or there.

15

"That's Monica. Fuck, Hitch, why didn't you tell me it was Monica." Rye said, holding the picture in his hand.

"Yeah, I kept it and sent Birdie home. He looked like a sweaty clam." Hitch replied.

"Are we still pretending we don't know about him and Monica? Their thing? His thing in hers?"

"No. We expressed our condolences."

"Shit." Rye looked at his feet, downtrodden. They were sitting around the camp burner Hitch used as a stovetop.

"Wait, isn't that Theo's mom?"

"Em, you know Christine?"

"Yeah, I live right there, dawg, did you forget?"

"Why didn't you say something earlier? Like when you met her?"

"Ya'll told me to act cool." DUH, written all over his face.

"Marcus," Salem was coming out of the bathroom, behind him the tub, "I live right there, too."

"Cracker wanna cookie?" Emcee rolled his eyes, he sounded like a retard, Rye pounded both their chests in laughter anyway.

"I'm saying I didn't see anything."

"No, you were on your high horse, motherfucker," Emcee barked.

"Only black guys say 'motherfucker' like that, you ever heard that one, Rye?" Salem started laughing along. "You got me, kid, for the racist piece of shit that I am. I like white people less than you and the Chinese less than anybody else. Those neanderthals from Nothern England really fuck with my mood, too."

"Stop avoiding the problem," Hitch cut in, deeply, "Emcee, get my box out of that cubbyhole behind you; we have to get high."

SOME TIME LATER.

"So this cop sneezes and I go, 'swine flu?'" Hank laughed along with his gang, all of them around Hitch's coffee table, on couch, chair, beanbag, whatever the fuck. "Yeah no, he hit me over the head and I spent quite a while in the home, fourteen was a rough year for me."

"What'd you do again?"

"The police caught me shitting on a cruiser. I tried to run but my shoe slipped on my poo and I landed face first on the pavement."

The group sat and talked like this for a long while. Good brainstorming always started with good conversation. Marcus was introduced to Ben, Hitch remained in his mask as Ben removed his.

"What do we do about Him?" Emcee asked

"Well, we need to find Him and then kill Him."

"He's looking for us though." Emcee said.

"Which means we let him come to us. Yes."

Everyone grew quiet and Hank turned on his television:

"The police still have no suspects. The pictures of the boy are posted online but we do not urge you to seek them out. They are disturbing. The lack of presence from a certain notorious group has not gone unnoted. Some are rumbling about how the heroes are good for nothing and others are wondering where our masked vigilantes were tonight.

The boy was stabbed with thirty-eight pieces of glass and this note was left pinned to his body. If anyone has any information please call the police right away, either by 9-1-1 or the direct hotline in the picture on your screen.

Of course, the tip hotline for our masked pedestrian overlords is still in service at star twenty-one.

Good night everyone. And good luck."

The man giving the special report was Asher Chase. He looked exactly what you'd expect of a man named Asher Chase: cool, slick-backed blonde hair, extraordinarily well placed stubble, slightly tan, hardened, with curious laughter hiding behind his eyes. A real woman's man.

The note hung on the screen again for a minute or two.

"Hector." Rye said.

"Somebody call him."

16.

"Shit, I can't really drive right now. No, no, that's fine I'll just walk. I'm gonna go get Theo, too. Alright. Yeah."

Sonofabitch assholedickhead when I get my hands on him. Thinking he could just come after me. Bring it on porkdick. Bring. It. On.

It was a brisk, thoughtful, walk over to Theo's. Monica's girls had been quick to set a system of watching Theo round the clock. Tonight Yasmin was slated to keep an eye, truthfully she'd end up needing both.

Knock Knock

"No!" Yasmin shrieked from within the house. "We said go away!"

"Theo."

"Hec?"

The door opened enough for a small black boy to peek his head in the crack. Through that same crack Hector had spotted the muzzle of a gun.

"Fuck you doing here?"

"You're not safe."

"Why you think I got this gun?" He paused. "You know who killed my mom?"

"Yes." Hector replied. "And no."

Theo let up, allowing Hector to enter his home. "Go on."

"He's coming after us. All of us. We don't really know why or how or anything really but he's sick. Fuck is this guy sick."

"Us?" Theo asked quizzically. "Like me and you? Is this cuz of that asswhoopin' ya'll gave to Elbows' crew?"

"No. I just need you to trust that we have to go. Now."

"I already got a bag packed. What took you so long, man? That nigga came up to my house dressed in black face and shit, just knocking. He'd leave and come back, drag his knife across the window. For a minute I thought he was gone so I looked out that window and the dude was waving and looking right at my window from the porch. That's when I got the gun. Scared the two of us to tits; Yas is about to give birth over there in the corner."

"That's insane."

"I know, bitch ain't even pregnant." Theo chuckled.

"Yasmin!" Hector called.

"What!"

"Go out the back door. Get out of here."

Hector turned the back lights on and watched Yasmin disappear in to the night.

Knock Knock

Hector made his way back to the front of the house and found Theo sitting and facing the front door, ready to shoot.

"Stay here." Hector said in a hush. "Take this back. Don't shoot unless I call for it. Got it?"

"Yeah."

Hector was smooth to the door, making not a sound. He opened it, slowly, expecting someone to try and bash through.

"Heather?"

"Hector."

"Oh sweet jesus; it's you."

The two exchanged curtsies as Theo ran up to embrace her, head coming to just below her bosoms. Water was already thick in her eyes and she let them pour the more when Theo showed his affection.

"He's dead." She sobbed. "Herald. And when I heard on Theo's mom…I just wanted to come make sure he was alright. I'm glad you're here, Hec." She said, going limp in his capable arms. "Did you hear about it?" She asked.

"Yeah."

"What happened?" Theo asked.

Laughter. Rough laughter rose—no fell—from one of the bedrooms in the ranch-style home.

"We had a slight mishap……Hector, would you mind telling the boy what happened?"

"Heather's boyfriend is dead. I'm assuming by your hand." Hector spoke into the darkness of a long hallway.

"Wouldn't you say it was more by your hand? Just like the boy's mother?"

"What's he talkin' about Hec?" Theo asked. Theo was scared shitless until he glanced up and saw that perhaps Hector wasn't one to be pushed into a corner like this, protecting people he loved.

"I'll tell you later." Hector sided out his mouth.

A figure could be seen sliding through the darkness. Hector reached for the light switch but it was on the other side of the hallway, tho he was not unprepared.

A smooth flashlight was pulled from one of his side pockets. He flipped a switch and the light strobed. The three could see the gnarly bastard coming at them in brief, photo-like, bursts of light. The strobe must have really disoriented the attacking man as he wobbled and met his face with Hector's fist. Hector shifted his strobing to where the man just crashed but he had disappeared into the darkness once more.

Heather screamed.

By now Theo was at the other end of the hallway and flipped the switch to the light on. No dice.

Theo thought quickly and clapped twice. Who knew a clap-on battery-powered lamp would come in handy?

Light illuminated the passageway and flooded into the living area. The painted man caught like a deer in headlights' light.

He quickly gathered-up Heather and put a knife to her throat. She was having none of that. She shrieked, he hesitated, and bit down on his hand with the force of a large pitbull. He dropped the knife, she gathered herself into a spinning back-handed punch.

Sidebar: Heather was a fan of the ultimate fighting scene. She worked out and sparred with large black men at the gym, it was well documented.

"Ya know." He said, getting up, clapping twice, and circling the three, "it's going to be a lot more fun killing you while you sleep."

Theo clapped again to illuminate the room but He was gone, somehow. They stayed at the ready for a few minutes, barely breathing, watching each corner of the house. Light and space breathing, every crick a face at the window.

Knock Knock

"Let's go! What are you guys doing?"

"Marcus?" Theo called to the door.

"Uhhh...no?" Emcee replied, queerly, from the other side of the door.

"You with anyone?" Hector called out.

"Yeah, me and Sales."

Hector nodded and Theo went to open the door. They were in uniform. Salem with his Katana and Emcee choosing a cool nine-millimeter, as well as two bats--uhhhhh metal and wood.

"Did you see him?" Theo asked.

"Who?"

"Our friend," Hector replied, haphazardly. "He was just here. Heather, you may want to come with us, too."

"Us?" Heather and Theo jinxed. They looked dumbfounded but deep in their bellies knew.

"Let's go." Hector said. "I'll tell you everything, but we have to go."

The five of them embarked for Rye's spacious homestead aware that their adversary could come out from any dark nook of space.

It did not take long to get to Rye's. The group filed in, barely knowing what was going on. They all took a seat and Hank, who elected to stay unhidden and wore only a robe, got them all a drink. Theo got a Coke. Hank put a little whiskey in it to help the kid out. Quarter shot.

Heather's sobbing had subsided and was replaced with silence. Her face was never more determined. Hector was the only one to notice this. She dared a glance at him and he stared at her with that same determination. He could see in her eyes how badly she wanted to press her body to his. The need to feel him inside her was in the forefront of her eyes. Shit, the need to feel anything better, good, really was. In fact, in them he could almost see her rump throwing itself back in hopeful anticipation of another inch or two, and feel her writhe as it was given.

Hector had to focus on something else, his erection becoming quite noticeable. What was it with tragedy that did this? Come closer, fuck me, I am feeling too much and alone.

"We've got to figure out what to do with this bastard." Hitch said after sometime.

"I don't know if we should be talking about it right now." Salem looked around and out a window, into the distance. "I don't trust that he's not watching us somehow."

"He's not." Hank replied. "I had George do a sweep earlier. No bugs, no nothing. Plus my phone will get an alert if any of the many cameras on the premises are called into action. The dogs would probably start going crazy. This guy would have to defy the laws of physics just to get within five-hundred fucks of this place." Just as Hank finished his statement the power for his entire mansion was cut and left off for a few seconds. As they glanced at each other, struggling to see for lack of light, laughter rang out.

Suddenly the lights re-illuminated, nothing was on the cameras. The dogs began to bark.

"Shit."

The rest of the night was quiet, with nothing but crickets and lapping water breaking the silence. The dogs did not bark, there was no more laughter. The night air stirred and blew just enough to make the house on the cliff feel more like the cool side of a pillow. All who stirred within felt drowsy from comfort and eventually gave in to the sleep they needed. Allowing the slow waves from below to roll through their own bodies. Theo, who thought he was last to be awake, was very close to wandering when that crazy, painted, face appeared behind his eyelids.

It's going to be a lot more fun to kill you while you sleep. He shuddered and jolted his eyes open.

"Hey," Hector whispered over to Theo. "Get some sleep."

17.

Marcus awoke, abruptly. He was on the floor, lying next to Heather—who *he* knew from the VIP section—and was still in full uniform, thus he was actually Emcee. It was already becoming quite the chore to discern between the two.

"Morning kid." Rye said from the kitchen. "How do you like your eggs?"

"Easy, overly so." Marcus replied, stretching out his limbs. "Black coffee if you got it."

"One Nubian coffee for my Nubian brother," poured Rye. "I bet you're wondering how I support all this."

"You think I wouldn't recognize Hank Green? How poor you think I am, man? Your name's on half the toilet paper in this country. Wouldn't put anything else on my asshole, bro."

"Comforting."

"It is though, shits plush. Where'd you get this coffee? Ecuador?"

"Colombia"

"Damn, it's good. Thank you."

Marcus sat and ate his breakfast. Hank did the same. The others grunted and stretched, eventually meeting Marcus and Hank in the kitchen, which was big enough to hold a party at least three times the size. Heather was still bra-less which was more than a treat for the bunch. They each drank coffee, Theo for his first time. They conversed for a short time over what might be a good plan for the day.

"Hector, could you show me where the towels are? I need to shower." Heather asked after conversation had died. Hector obliged without hesitation.

Today would not be sunny and bright. The clouds looked heavy—like they needed wrung out—and began to take their places so that electricity might be passed between them. Ben and Theo stood at one of the many large windows overlooking the cliff, water down there some ways sloshed around, and the stone pillars a thousand yards stood and swayed with a roaring wind. Water slammed into the rocks below with vehement force.

"No boats out there today." Said Ben, mainly to himself.

"Did you know my mom, too?" Theo asked.

"Yes," Ben said to the boy. "She was a lovely woman. She helped us catch many of the sickos around here."

"Is that why he killed her?"

"I don't know, probably."

Theo sunk into his shoulders and continued looking out towards the coming storm. Marcus got up from his chair and walked over to join the two. He stood next to, and placed his arm around, Theo. Droves of rain chucked on the glass separating them from the elements. The droplets slid down the glass and eventually met up, forming tiny rivers that only grew in size. Words to console Theo could not find Marcus' lips nor tongue. Ben stood entranced with the squall and was no doubt wrestling with his mind to understand how he could portray such violent beauty. Awe is meant for more than two eyes, one mind. *Behold everything greater than you; stand in awe of it.*

"Is it in the details or the tone?"

"What?" Marcus asked Ben, arm still around Theo.

"Nothing."

"It's the tone," Marcus said, realizing what Ben was getting at.

"The storm rages so that flowers may bloom."

Hank chucked an orange at Ben's back from across the kitchen. "Will you stop? You're trying too hard. Besides, we have shit to do."

Theo could not keep quiet any longer. "All of you stop. Talking about tone and flowers and shit while my mom's killer is probably prancing around laughing in the rain like a fucking fairy." Theo's stomach was in his throat, his face red hot. "Not to mention tweedle's dee and dumb up there humping in the shower. Is this how you guys deal with things? Eat a nice meal, ponder rain storms, bed women. Let's just hide out here and hope he doesn't kill anyone or come get us."

"Easy Thee." Marcus said while squeezing the boy. Theo flung out of Marcus' grip.

"No. I'm done. I've had it with you pansies."

"Theo." Hitch said, making an entrance from the other room. "We'll get him. You know what he's after right now?"

"A response,"

"yes, a response. He's not doing things in broad daylight. We need to play this out. Someone else may die."

"You could always give yourself up, motherfucker."

"They win now, they do for the rest of times."

"And your cause is so just? Bring up the greater good one time. See if I can't cite at least eight instances of it being used by a fucking lunatic. There is no greater good,"

"only the man next to you. I know. Look at us, Thee. Understand *you* are the greater good. The rest of us only hope not to fuck it up."

18.

Later on in the day Marcus' phone rang in his pocket. He took it out and said hello.

'What's the word, Zee?'

'You all good for tonight?'

With all that had gone on Marcus forgot about Zee, as well as their endeavor, scheduled for this very evening. Marcus found his way to one of the many empty rooms in Hank's house before speaking again.

'Tonight isn't going to work.'

'Oh, well let me tell that to George. Mr. Hammer, I know we owe you a bunch of money and that you've killed for lesser amounts, but tonight just doesn't work. Could we maybe do next Tuesday?'

'Alright, I get it.'

'Oh you're booked next Tuesday? Well let's see here. I could possibly fit a heist in two weeks from Monday."

'Alright.' Marcus said, clearly growing agitated.

'I'm sorry man. This whole situation has me twelve different kinds of fucked up. Just be here by eight,' Zee bid, hanging up.

Marcus cursed and punched a wall. It felt good so he punched another.

The day wore on. Plans were discussed, thrown out, and then revisited. Hector and Heather disappeared once or twice. Theo spent the whole of the day sitting in a chair, staring out a window at the never ending storm—which had rumbled all through breakfast, lunch, and now looked as though it would through dinner, tho now more sultry than chaotic. The droplets being let go put Theo in a mindless trance. He did not hear Butler come up behind him.

"Hello young sir. Dinner will be soon. How do you take your steak?"

"Up your ass, bitch." Theo replied, still in his chair.

"No one tells the butler a thing but the butler knows and hears the stories." Butler said pulling a stool from over somewhere, bringing it next to Theo. "My own mother told me something once. 'Now one day I will be gone. Whether it is by the hand of a god or a man I do not know. You will carry on, But.' She liked to call me But. She's a funny woman. 'You will carry on because that is all your mother ever wanted, for you to do well and be kind.'"

"How did your mother die?"

"She didn't. But the lesson remains the same."

"My mom always told me that if I ever got to eat steak I should order it medium rare."

"She sounds like a smart woman." Butler rose and placed the stool back where it was. He turned to leave and paused. "One of these wretched days you will get an opportunity, and you should take it. Redemption outweighs revenge on every metric."

19

"What do you guys think of that George Hammer character?" Marcus wolfed down the last of his steak. Over various and well-seasoned courses, conversation managed to dwindle around the soft clink of silverware to plate.

"Why do you ask?" Hitch wondered.

"He is scuzz." Ben chimed. "He tells us the information he wants, nothing more."

"We keep relatively good tabs on him, though. Usually, anyway. Over these past few days we haven't had much a chance to pry." Hitch said.

"What do you mean, Ben?" Marcus asked.

"What I mean is that we hope he is on our side, but we don't really know. He might keep tabs on us the same way we do him."

"Would he have any idea who we are? You know, really?" Marcus looked at all of them, wondering if they were in on it, somehow, a test of sorts.

Hitch sighed and his face became defeated. "Normally I'd say no, but I'm not so sure anymore. Hopefully he's alive long enough for us to find him tonight. This is all shit."

"Would He know who I am?" Marcus asked

"Who? George?"

"No, blackface." Marcus wanted to talk about George, but, thought it best to focus on something else. "It seems like He's been casing you guys out but may not know who I am. He may not even know you guys have a new member."

"He may not." Hitch said, intrigued, mind free-wheeling.

20.

Dusk was settling in as Rye and Birdie hooked off State street and into an alley betwixt a few closed shops. An extremely handsome and dashing man stood in the alleyway to meet them.

"Asher," Rye sounded as if he were greeting an old friend.

"Rye, Birdie." Asher Chase responded with a slight nod to his head. "Did the band break-up?"

"The others are checking elsewhere."

"For the man who killed that boy?"

"Yeah."

"Have any luck?"

"Sort of.

"Oh?"

"I don't really know where to start."

"Out with it man. Just tell me what's up."

"He's a guy. All we know right now is that He is trying to get rid of us."

"Us being whom?"

"Me, Birdie, anyone else who wears a mask at night to keep this town quiet. He was in my house a few nights ago. Drugged me and then the next morning sent me a video of him shouting at my unconscious body, don't know why he didn't just kill me...He's visited us a few other times, too." Rye paused, waiting for some kind of response from Asher, who gave none. "He killed one of our other informants already. Cut up her body and sent us a picture."

"Yeah, I heard about Christine. I figured the dots connected there. I saw you guys talking to her from time to time. Didn't she have a kid?"

"Yeah he's safe. We have him."

"Damn, he must be in some kind of shape."

"He's not in a good place. None of us are. This guy is twisted. We have a description but no identity yet. We know he knows my identity, and Birdie's." Rye said glancing over at Birdie who stood as a statue. "But we don't know if he knows anyone else's, though we are going under the assumption that he does."

"Give me what you can, I'll report it."

Rye nodded. "Right. Then you should probably go somewhere safe. We're getting a safehouse established and will let you know where it is if you'd like. Have you heard anything from your end?"

"Just bogus tips. Keep your ear to the news though. When there's news. There's Asher." Asher chuckled lightly. "Ahhh shit. What have you got for me?"

"Well, he is a large man. He's got neck length hair that looks like it's never been groomed, slick black, gnarly."

"Anything that would make him stand out?"

"I'd say so. He doesn't wear a shirt and has the entire upper half of his body covered in black paint."

"Black face. Could this be race related?"

"We think it more likely that this guy is nuts enough to roll around in black paint, or tar or something, I don't know. Probably lead based too. Crazy fucker."

"Alright, I gotta get to the station. You got the burner phone on you?"

"Yeah."

"I'll let you know if we get anything."

"Sounds good."

Rye and Birdie began to walk back out into the street and Asher called to them. "Hey Rye, I hope this guy likes foot in his rectum!"

"My foot!!!" Rye called back as he disappeared around a corner.

21.

"George, can we trust you?" Hitch asked it simply. The two met after Hitch had checked all George Hammer's usual spots of patronization, finally finding him smoking outside of a bar. A bar named Bernie and Jets.

"That's a little insulting." George labored through noisy breathes. "What have I ever done to dissuade you of my honesty?"

"You mean besides all your little side projects you tell us nothing about?"

"Insinuating is for assholes."

"Yeah, well so is being an actual asshole. We know you set up heists from time to time at businesses you are protecting." Hitch used air quotes to make his last word punch.

"Alright, alright. I know you guys have some bigger problems so I'll stop being one."

"Do you know anything about our guy?"

"Jesus, no, that guy seems like a psychopath. I make a few bucks on the side every here and then. I don't let killers loose."

"You got anything for tonight that we don't know about?"

"Nope."

Hitch studied the sweaty fat man before him. The sweaty fat man took a puff and flicked his cigarette into the street.

"Good. Stay aware tonight Georgie. This guy we're chasing is a real sick son of a bitch."

"You do the same. I'll be here if you need anything."

George turned and went back into the bar. The back of his pants scrunched up into his ass as if his cornhole were trying to eat them. Hitch shook his head and chuckled, continuing on. Night had fallen and Hitch did not want to be caught alone, not this evening.

He met up with Rye and Birdie on one of the side streets off State. The two were all in a huff.

"Radio. 3rd." Rye said as he sucked in oxygen.

"What?" Hitch asked.

Birdie came to before Rye could catch his wind. "There's a robbery over on third."

"Let me guess." Hitch said. "One of Hammer's places?"

"Yeah."

"Son of a bitch."

"Yeah."

The men stood around for a moment deciding what to do with such a conundrum. They could either stand here all night and forget about the capes they kept, or they could hunt down their painted psychopath, or they could fancy to go to third street to meet whatever plan George Hammer had set for them.

"Let's head over. No use having dicks if we can't swing 'um."

22

"Decoy robbery?" Marcus asked. Pulling a ski-mask over his face. His body was flying down State street at forty-five miles an hour. He was, of course, entrapped in a motor vehicle.

"Yeah, a few guys holding up a small store on third. George called the tip in early. Anyone decides to head there is practically walking in to a trap."

"Or running."

"What?"

"Nothing."

Zee held a curious gaze on Marcus for a moment, then opened his door. He hollered for the driver to circle around the block one time, two times if they didn't run out immediately after the once. Zee glanced back at Marcus, both stomping out of the long vehicle, Marcus met the young producer's eyes and nodded.

Glass doors broke under the weight of their crowbars. The two entered with hurried assurance, not a shard of glass piercing their black skin. The video surveillance system was offline, but the alarm still sounded. Marcus ran ahead of Zee and bashed in every glass casing he could find before returning to grab the diamonds; drained of any sparkle because of the night.

The car outside the store went to make its first pass. The driver of the vehicle stopped in front for naught a moment. His ears perked up as he was aware of a slight hum cutting through the sound of sirens: wailing distant and stationary.

"Cops aren't on their way, we could probably grab all of it. Take 'um a few minutes to drive here if they even come." Zee proclaimed, grabbing a tangerine sized bit of carbon and throwing it into his bag.

"It's not the cops I'm worried about."

"Why is the car parked out front?"

"What?"

A man wearing an odd, silk like, mask sprant from a dark part of the store and forced himself on Zee while also forcing Zee to the ground. Marcus recognized the man's garb, he knew the mask all too well.

Marcus anticipated the man coming from the corner to his back. Wolves hunted in packs, but once a hare learns the tactics of the wolves a hare can avoid sharp fangs.

Marcus ducked as Birdie flew over his back and decided he ought to flee. His sprint for the back was met by a forceful fist to his gut.

"I hope your colon likes steel-toed boot."

Marcus coughed, "Asshole." He wavered while holding his gut for a second and finally brought his own fist up straight into Rye's jaw. Rye spit after the blow.

"You should have used that crowbar." He said.

Rye went in to maul Marcus when a single shot boomed itself into existence. Rye dropped and slumped like spittle on a burger.

Marcus had never thought himself a coward, but still he slammed the back door open and zigzagged his way to a vacant and empty parking lot. The only light-pole stood flickering in the middle of the setup. The moon's light could not reach this spot. The air seemed more eerie. Marcus stopped for a moment to try and ponder something that soon left his grasp. He could hear footsteps closing in behind him. There were buildings all around the car park save for one side, his only exit route.

Marcus started to run. The opposite side of the parking lot seemed to be light-years away. He'd make it though. Just…a…little.

"Ow!" Marcus yelled. The pain was small, like a prick, but instantaneously the kid felt woozy, like his legs had decided not to take any calls from his spinal cord. He still had momentum so he flailed forward until tripping up and meeting his nose to the hard concrete.

He came out of the shadows. What little remained of Marcus' vision could see that. Marcus worked all his might just to try a push up. Nothing. His arms wouldn't move, lousy fucking things. Where had He gone? Marcus felt himself melting into the ground.

A hard hand jerked his collar back.

As his vision tunneled to nothing he was being dragged across a sea of pavement, there was a point out there, if he could reach it Marcus knew he'd be alright. He reached, watching the point grow further, less focused. He imagined with all his might that he were jerking around and screaming in hopes it would force his body to do so. It did not.

The skies opened up again, Marcus was out cold. Our man with the long hair slid him in a sewer, was gone himself.

23.

"I can't get ahold of Emcee." Hitch said. Tossing his pre-paid phone to the dumpster.

"Maybe he just fell asleep. You did tell him to take the night off." Birdie replied.

"No. I don't like the feel of this."

The fluorescent lighting around the two burned their eyes. They would have burned Rye's too, had they been open. The room was small and dank. Water pipes shot through the ceiling and an IV dripped slowly into Rye's arteries. He lied there. A man hurriedly entered the room.

"I'm going to need to keep him for observation." The man said, putting his hands on his hips, flailing the tail of his white coat.

Hitch addressed him. "Doc, we can't keep him here."

"Take him then. He woke up for five minutes and asked where the stick was."

"What stick?"

"The one up my ass."

Rye let out a muffled and painful chuckle at this.

"Oh good," Doc said. "He's awake."

"What's up Doc? You find that stick?" Rye tried not to sound in pain, Bird cringed watching him make the attempt.

"Should've left that bullet in you, Hank."

"Oh, go sit on a cactus."

The Doc hit a button, smirking, Rye fell back to sleep.

116

"Anyway, he's not in good shape. His vitals are all over the place and I'm fairly sure a piece of the bullet is still floating around in there somewhere."

"Is anyone going to find him down here?" Hitch asked.

"In the basement of a bookstore?" The Doc laughed. "No, no I don't think anyone will. Go take care of what you need to, Hitch, I'll keep an eye on him. Say, you got any weed?"

Hitch tossed him a small bag and motioned for Birdie to exit.

Birdie stood outside, Hitch had a word or two with the Doc. Exited.

"Birdie?" Hitch asked

"Yeah."

"What are we going to do?"

"Kill the fucker."

"They'll hate us. It's obvious; we weren't around, he wouldn't be either."

"You don't know that. Besides, if it was our fault it would still be on us to rectify it anyway, at the very least."

They walked for a minute, perhaps two. Who's to know, none of it is real. "Why, because 'he'd win,' or 'evil would win?' Fuck you, Hitch. People are dying. You're scared shitless that you won't have a purpose without this. And you are willing to kill me, and everyone, so that you can live on in posthumous, anonymous, glory. Be a fucking movie someday or some shit. You know who is most loved, remembered? Jesus fucking Christ, asshole. And he was crucified. We're all so brainwashed that we still think yours the righteous path. No one even brings up the solution that would really end this. Your solution ends with at least another eight people dead,

Andrew. Wrap that around your cornrows. Let something penetrate that thick skull of yours for once."

Hitch cracked Bird on the back of the head, Bird gasped, reached for his head. "I told you, motherfucker! I tell all of you!"

Bird landed one to Hitch's gut, "you paranoid fucking twat. You're delusional! You live in a comic book 24/7!" Hitch stopped clutching his gut, Bird hit him again. "It's all our fault!" Bird wailed, repeating the phrase, eventually punching the walls, they were in some alley, only rats to hear them. "It's all our fault!" He kicked a few dumpsters, rage, rage, rage. Like every young prophet out there Bird kicked and punched, fighting destiny until it gave him an absent tooth.

Hitch was slumped against some garbage and slimy disposal, shaking off the anger in him. Understanding with an, 'aha, of course!' attitude, watching Bird flop and howl.

24.

Theo lay in Heather's lap staring at the ceiling fan. Round, the blades swirled and Theo caught a blade, dragged his eyes along with it, seeing how long he could keep up. Wuhwuhwuhwuh. Round and round, while Ben was unmasked, pacing forth and back again. Heather made sure the baseball bat she brought in remained in her sights. Ready to be grabbed and used. She knew what to do with hard wood.

Birdie and Hitch trudged in through the foyer, under a crystalline chandelier, and through double doors leading to a screened in porch. Thunderheads plumed in the distance but shrank across the vast lake before them. Ben peeked up from his book and looked curiously down at the raging waters below.

"Billion yeared rock knocker." He thought aloud.

"What?"

"Have you ever read such a thing?" Ben chuckled to himself and repeated the line a few more times. "And suddenly I feel like a shitty writer again."

"That's because you are a shitty writer, Ben. Don't take it personally tho. You all are. Is Marcus here?" Hitch asked.

"No." Said Ben.

"Shit."

"What?"

"He wasn't at home either. Won't answer his phone."

"Shit. Where's Hank?"

"Bookstore."

"What?"

"*THEE* bookstore, Ben."

"Oh. OH! He okay?"

"Doc Rivera is keeping him for observation. So long as he doesn't try to crack any jokes he should live."

"Hank? No shit. I heard about the jeweler heist on the radio. They think one got away."

"One did."

"The other?"

"I'm not sure. Cops got there right as we were about to pulverize him."

The news was interrupted in the other room for breaking coverage. Asher Chase's low, charismatic, voice could be heard from the porch.

"In breaking news we have a description of the man who brutally murdered a boy last night outside of the Pompadour movie theatre. The man is tall and with long hair. He wears no shirt and from the waste up is covered in black ink. Even his face. He is believed to be killing at random and with no motive. This man is extremely dangerous. If you see him call 9-1-1 before you call our tip line."

"Bullshit, no motive." Theo proclaimed.

"Theo if people knew why they might…"

"…what, hate you?"

"C'mon Thee. It's bad enough that this guy is looking for us. You want the whole town on our asses?"

"Kind of." Theo said with a grin. "Bring out the pitchforks."

"Thee."

"Fuck you and your 'Thee' shit. If you weren't humping my mom she'd still be alive."

Hector hushed up. Lightning struck the lake off in the distance.

"We've got to find Marcus." Hitch said.

25.

Hector woke up next to Heather. Filling her hole(s) was starting to lose its grandeur. He watched her break a smile and open her eyes.

"Hey." She said.

"Hey yourself, lady."

"How are you? Your eyes look funny. Funny sad."

They had taken up sleeping in Hank's luxurious sheets while he was away.

"I just…with everything going on I've hardly had time to miss Monica."

"Oh."

"I just think she deserves more. More than me humping away while her killer struts around."

"I know. I've almost forgotten entirely about Herald. I didn't go to his funeral."

"Monica didn't even have one."

"Oh."

"Yeah."

"I like you, Hector."

"You like my cock."

"Why can't I like your cock, too?" She asked, placing her hand on it. "Wake up little guy." She lightly patted his whacker.

"Hey."

"Sorry. Wake up tiny fella!"

"That's it!" Hector yelled as he threw himself on top of her. She squealed as he dug his face into her belly. The smoothness of the sheets was enough to make her nipples hard. His tongue slowly finding its way down was enough to make her wet.

"Hey," She said, "come up here a minute."

"Not a chance, lady, I don't want this thing to dry up." Hector emerged from under the sheets and took Heather's face in his hands. "What?"

"Why does this moment seem so terrific?"

"Because your mind is ringing with hormones. Bells upon bells of vibrating, earth shattering, force, ponging through your lobes."

Knock Knock

"Let's go." Hitch said, exploding through the bedroom door. "And get that blood rushing back to your head...err...brain. We've got to go get Rye."

"Already? Did you find Marcus?"

"I was out all night, didn't find shit. Doc's got a shift to do at the hospital. Says Hank's well enough."

"The sun's not even up yet."

"Precisely. My. Motherfuckin. Point. Now put your dingaling away and let's get the fuck out of here."

"Dingaling?" Heather laughed to herself. She relinquished Hector from her vice like grip and began looking around the room for something else she could use. She watched man become hero. His broad hard muscles somehow looked more refined as they slid into the black, seemingly seamless, piece of fine material that stretched from his feet to his neck. Kevlar

123

stood guard and was sewn in to different sections of the suit: chest and abs, shoulders, thighs (outside), and shins.   There was also a small piece protecting the achilles'—just in case.

"Take the sharp ones." Hitch said from out the door.

Hector picked up a carbon-fiber vest and placed it over his shoulders. The back pouches already had his weapon(s) of choice strapped on.   A long, reinforced looking and night black, axe crossed his back and at both sides of the slanted axe were two smaller, but still large, axes. He threw on a black utility belt, filling it with an array of fine gadgets, weapons.

"And the grenades." Hitch shouted in.

Hector grabbed two pea-colored tangerines from out of Hank's closet and pouched them. He put on a thicker pair of pants which looked as bulky as snow-slacks, and then put on his dark boots. Heather had held them just last night and damned if they weren't the lightest shoes she'd ever lifted.

"Punch me in the leg." Hector requested.

Heather got up and worked all her might into a punch that hit Hector's leg and did nothing. In fact, Heather's fist was absorbed in to his pants and the blow made tiny rippling waves up and down his leg like a lava lamp. His pants seemed to be made of liquid foam.

"Shoot my leg." He said with a grin.

Heather went to reach for the gun on the nightstand.

"No!" Hector shouted. "I was joking, woman!" He kissed her as he slid on his mask.

"Be safe." Said she.

"No." Said he.

26.

As Hitch and Birdie approached the bookstore they could see ambulances hurrying into the emergency bay on the other side of the street. Too many to be normal.

27.

There Is a Serial Killer in Trident: Be Cautious

An article by Asher Chase

There are many wild speculations, articles and rumors running amuck at this moment. Please understand that I am taking information I trust and trying to explain what is going on to you in a manner which presents what happens, without making you biased towards whatever I feel to be true. In other words, think for yourself. Understand what is happening and know it to be serious.

We are told that Herald Yolk was waiting for his girlfriend in the parking lot. Friends had told him not to wait for "his hoe" too much longer as they left him in said parking-lot. Alone.

In the course of someteen minutes Herald had been brutally stabbed thirty-seven times with pieces of his window and various bits of his windshield. His body was left in the parking lot where dozens of half-frightened teens emerged after surviving a viewing of "Halloween Night: The Return." Coincidences are just numbers that smash together.

His killer left a note. You can read its contents in the photograph below.

Herald was not the man's target—I say a man of course because I have some new intel I'll be sharing—in fact, allegedly someone named Hector Bridge was. When we asked the teens surrounding the scene what they made of the note a few had this to say:

"Yeah, Cornelius, that kid looks just like that dude. And his name is Hector. Works up at the community center."

"I heard Herald's girlfriend ditched his ass at the movies and got drinks with Hector."

"Yeah they definitely got it on."

So by any accounts we assume the man in question, and in danger, as Hector Cornelius Bridge. He looks just like Herald. He was not at work today--which should not have surprised me--so I did not get a quote from him nor am I aware of his whereabouts. His parents live all the way out in Pawtucky so they should be fine. Herald's girlfriend, Heather Raulston, has also been missing.

Police and hero forces alike believe the murder of Christine Mathis is in connection with the stabbing of Herald Yolk.

Sometime in the night on the 24th Christine was abducted, though she was not known to be missing until a picture was delivered to her son. On that picture was Christine's dismembered body arranged in an I-Spy like game. Her son, Theo Matthis, has since been missing. I'm told he is under protection. The picture of Christine Matthis is being held by the police and cannot be published.

Now of course there are various forces pursuing this man. Those both government funded, and vigilante. The police offered us no insight while an "anonymous source" gave me a description of the killer: White male(sort of), tall, "ape-armed" said the source, long unwashed hair, and black ink covering his body from the waist up through his face. Usually this man is seen without a shirt and will, again, just be covered in ink or an ink-like substance.

Could this be a racially motivated escapade? No, probably not.

The speculations will rage like waters against tuna; I certainly have mine. Regardless of what half-witted reporters will tell you, there are certain truths we know at this moment. This man is dangerous. This man is crazed. And this man will not hesitate to hurt anyone. I recommend traveling in pairs, droves even, and being inside your homes come nightfall.

I will be continuing my search for knowledge enough to give you, the people, beit day or night.

28.

The makeshift hospital room was empty save for the various medical machines and the bed. The TV was also still in the room. So, it wasn't really empty at all I suppose, just missing Hank.

A remote lay on the night-side-table and had a little note ("Turn me on!").

"Shit." Hitch said.

"Double shit." Birdie said.

"Why did we leave him here again?"

Birdie shrugged. "It seemed like a good idea. Why can't we take this seriously?"

"Should have been here."

"Or should have brought him back."

"Shit."

"I don't want to do it."

"Nor I."

"Turn it on, Hitch."

The TV clicked, showing brightly; there were no going back.

Marcus sat in a room by himself on the opposite side of the screen. The room looked as though it were in a warehouse somewhere. His head hung in insignificance.

"It looks like they're here." Some voice away from the camera said. "Ya know, you guys really picked a bad time to look for new members."

"Fuck you." Birdie said to the television.

The screen remained unchanged in silence for moments, holding on Marcus' drooping head. Suddenly a song came cawing through the television speakers and Marcus perked up, familiar with the tune and his own voice.

A large figure became visible behind Marcus. The figure swayed and playfully jived along to the beat of the song, wiggling fingers and hips in soulful cohesion. The speakers boomed.

He did a few short steps behind Marcus before going to his left and right, all the while spinning his feet and wobbling his knees.

"Is that the chicken dance?" Hitch asked no one, watching the screen with his head tilted and concern on his face.

Almost in response the figure—who is indeed the inked antagonist—snapped back to the camera. At this point Marcus saw the knife in His hand and started his own form of gyration: the "get out of these shackles" swing.

The man took His place behind the struggling Marcus and flashed the knife for the camera to see.

"You wanna dance?" He asked, coldly, filleting Marcus' neck until blood poured from a dozen tiny rivers. Birdie had to look away, Hitch too. Though they could still hear Marcus gurgling on his own fluids.

Hitch shut it off and set the room on fire. This were an old building, made mostly of wood and other various blocks of flammability. Also, the books.

Men and women from the hospital across the street had begun to run over to see if the building held any wounded; Or maybe to loot a book or two. Our heroes slipped out the back door.

They ran off into the shadows hiding in the alleys, eventually making it to taller buildings.

"What now?" Birdie asked between strides.

"Dirt bikes." Hitch said with a grin. "Better to be mobile if we're out in broad daylight."

29.

A man walked as the slow wooing of a train ate his ears whole. It sped by him, missing by a mere foot or two. He wondered about how something moving that fast could not run directly off the track. There is a restaurant up the road. What genius decided to put it directly in the way of a hypothetically-derailing train? This monstrosity might run clear over it and right on to the highway.

He lit up a cigarette and sat on a train that was immobile, falling apart. A gentleman, who was much older and wearing an all-black tuxedo, moved with the gracefulness of a man who had mastered the art of walking, and brought himself to face the smoke of his companions cigarette.

"Are you done groveling in the trainyard, sir?"

"Are you done being rhetorical?"

"Technically, sir…"

"…Yes, I know it would only be rhetorical if it were obvious that I was done groveling in the train yard. Which it is not because I just lit up a cigarette."

"So this conversation is useless because it is obvious that you are not, in fact, done groveling?"

"Well, yes."

"Hm."

"Hm."

"Anyway, shall we dress your wounds, sir?"

"No."

"Well can I at least get that knife out of your back, sir?"

"No."

"Right. Well then I suppose there's nothing to do but bleed out in the middle of nowhere surrounded by abandoned trains."

"That son-of-a-whore came for me, Butler. While I was asleep no less. He would have gotten away with it if he weren't such a little fucking bitch."

"A cunt really."

The funny talking man in the tuxedo walked off on his own.

The train that was passing did so in succession and the pudgy patrons of the pizza place were safe for another hour and seventeen minutes. The rest of the landscape was also uninhibited, and brilliantly so. John Log's Pizza Cabin was stuck in the wilderness as a lone button on a quilt. Even the old trainyard seemed a part of it all.

You know how the wind sounds when walking under a birch and the birdsong practically jumps into your mind, giving you a tune to whistle?

Another train wooed well off in the distance, vibrating and ricocheting from tree to tree, shaking the roots. He reached and pulled the knife from his back. His face scrunched so much it looked like it would disappear. He let out but a grunt.

"Butler!" He called.

"Sir?"

"Find my phone. And dress these fucking wounds already. I'm going to bleed out, if I don't get devoured by maggots."

"You were being quite stubborn sir."

"And what have I said?"

"Even if you're being stubborn, always dress the fucking wounds."

"Verbatum. Now dress. Phone first."

30.

We're all here now. We're all in the grand space of Hank's living room. All of us except Marcus, oh, and Hank. Theo Mathis was upstairs crying and playing video games; now he's on the couch; he's eating grilled cheese. Heather was in her nude and was thinking on Hector and if he was safe, then Hector came and how pleased she was when she heard his boots hit the wood of Hank's floors. Hitch had them meet in the living room we find ourselves in now. They sat around and listened to Theo munch. They stunk of bad news and no one wanted to ask what it was.

"Where's your boy?" Theo asked, between bites.

"We don't know, Theo." Hitch said, not really paying attention to the words as he said them.

Theo half grinned and took another bite. "Ya'll said you was going to get him. So where is he Hitch? Where is he, *Hector*?"

"We don't know, Thee." Hector said, slipping off his mask.

"Eh, maybe he'll do you a solid and box Hank's ass up like those steaks the mother fucker got in there. Send um here. Maybe he'll put them around town and ya'll stupid niggas can go on a treasure hunt or some shit. NOW, WHERE IS. YOUR BOY HECTOR?!" Theo was standing and yelling and Heather reached up, pulling him down and close.

"Hello!!!" Hank yelled, smashing through the doors. "Somebody pour me a drink."

"Pour it yourself!"

"Who said that?" Hank asked, coming around the corner from the hallway. He was bloody and wrapped in gauze. The sun shown through the windows, soft and orange. No one answered. Hank grinned. "Fuck you guys." He said, half chuckling.

"Got it!" Ben said, coming from the other end of the hallway, handing Hank a drink. "Jesus you look like shit. What's going on?"

"Ben were you here…?"

"Here all day? Yeah, writing. Why? What's up?"

"Seriously?"

"No. Hank it's good to see you, now dish. What happened? I heard you got kidnapped but my money was on you running off. What's with the blood? Is that a knife wound?"

"Shut the fuck up, Ben."

So then Hank got to explaining. It is quite the long story which went a lot like this: He came for Hank and succeeded, Hank woke up in a building, fought Him off, and as he left he walked through a room where Marcus was flopped on the floor in a dried pool of his own blood. The small room reminded Hank of a petri dish filled with disgusting ooze.

"He got away." Hank said. "Truth be told he's probably in better shape than I am now."

Hitch went to explaining he and Hec's time in the bookstore.

"What the fuck is happening?" Hitch asked. His voice was defeated and genuinely quizzical.

Hector rose first and embraced the old man. Theo walked on his legs as though they were full grown and joined the two. Ben felt his soul stir and move him to join, Hank will say that he felt obligated but his soul stirred, too. Heather was the last to join the circle, and was met with kind and defeated arms, placing herself under them.

What does the night bring with its darkness that makes the ghouls come out? What gravity does the moon pull with? Does it pull the tides or the madness? A dark rock with feaux light, large enough for us to feel its weight, alone in orbit around where it came from. The moon shown brightly through the living room window because a crater catapulted it to space long before it had windows to shine through.

"You remember where He took you?" Theo asked from the middle of the shell.

"Yeah." Hank said.

31

Well they'd be coming, because that is what the over-aggressive do. That's what He assumed would happen. He'd never heard the one about the verb that would make an ass of him.

His broken mirror reflected his bathroom, which consisted of a pipe running from inside the window to the outside, a box, and a few plastic barrels of water. There was also a drain in the middle of the floor.

He kicked the box over and stuck his dick in the window pipe, pissed through it. He grabbed one of the barrels and doused himself with water, after which he added another fist-sized hole in the wall. He walked out buck naked and over to the middle of his main warehouse room. He put his balls on the face of the young black man who was slumped on the floor. He cackled and jerked off on the man's face. It wasn't nearly as satisfying as skull fucking the prostitute. His hair dripped and clung together in vine-like fashion. Lice probably swung from one vine to another. The room was also dripping and probably hid many a bug.

"And I quote." He said, addressing the nigger with cum on his face. "'What really keeps me breathing?' Well, mister lyrical genius. It is your diaphragm. The answer we were looking for was, the diaphragm. Let's see, hmmmm." He read through the cover of some album case and pondered. Pointing and tssking. He was fairly judgmental. "Existentially, I don't see how this non-inspired droll could ever rise above mediocrity. Nor do I see how making one's fiscal means known makes you any more of a decent citizen than your average homeless man. If I had my dictionary with me I could use some other very large words to describe how I feel about these songs." He thought for another second or two. "But I suppose I am a bit riled up from the content, which is probably what you were going for. Laughing when other's get mad and all." He threw the album. "Not like any of it helped you, you know. Now." He laughed and pranced around a bit. His body was black from the waist up. His penis was still fairly erect.

He shook out until he was dry and put on a large overcoat, a hat and went to leave before pausing, thinking. With maniacal strides he dumped over a few bins, lighting the gasoline in them.

32.

Knock Knock

She was busy cooking a bit of bacon. Knocks at her door oft made her nervous. But, through the eyehole was no more than a tiny man with a tool belt. She'd seen him around her apartment complex. He'd waved to her a few times.

"I have to change the batteries on your lock," he said when she granted him entrance, "sorry."

"Ok."

"Yeah, because they might die."

"Ok, yeah, sure, thank you."

"Thank you, sorry."

The man was being sheepish and coy. All five-foot five of him shook and begot uneasiness. He was in all of about twenty seconds, and then out. He did ask her to use her own fab to ensure it worked, and it did. She shut the door behind him and went about her business. The bacon was done. Her small apartment was warmed with its aromas.

He left her apartment descended the stairs and left out the door to the parking garage. There was another man smoking under one of the flickering lights over by the garbage cans. The small man strode over and lit a cigarette of his own. His eyes darted like he was expecting everything at every moment.

"Don't forget to copy the pictures for me." He said, in broken English.

"I won't"

"And her panties?"

"Deal."

"Two pair?"

"Yeah."

The two men exchanged a small fab, much like the one the girl upstairs would use to unlock her apartment. The taller of the two was much taller and equal parts caucasion and toothsome, he received the fab with zest and examined it coolly. The day had barely begun and already the man couldn't wait for the night's excursion.

He was going to leave, but she came out of the garage door the way the small man had. She strode over and took a long drag. How delightful for him. A moment which should not be wasted.

"Hi, I'm sorry," said the tall man, "do you live here?"

She turned to him and he saw the familiarity spring to her face. "Yeah, I do. You're that guy I always see on the news."

"Guilty," he said, grinning and extending his hand. "Asher Chase."

"Hannah," she said, "Hannah Storm."

"Huh. Well I've got to get to the station but maybe I'll see you later on, Hannah Storm. Adieu."

The small man was trying to hide that he was staring at the buxom Hannah Storm as he shook profusely. Once Asher left; it was just the two of them.

"Are you okay?" Hannah asked.

He tried to look at anything but her and put his cigarette on the ground, walked away. It almost sounded like the man was scolding himself under his voice. What a strange little imbecile.

She went back in and decided the rest of the day would be spent with her television and then her bed.

She sat there for hours like she liked to, losing herself and her time to the tube. Eventually it would be time to wash up and get the teeth brushed, maybe pull out her vibrating little friend from the top drawer, and rest. What a mood seeing the handsome Asher Chase had put her in. The smile of a man who wanted her was quite the aphrodisiac. Maybe she would see him again. She had to dish, and not just with anyone. She pulled out her phone:

"Hey, Heather, what's up?"

"Yeah still at the lakehouse? That is great." She wanted to act like she cared because she had her reason for calling, "uh-huh, yeah, sounds great. Hey, you'll never guess who I ran into today…no not her, dirty cunt…no. Asher Chase. Yeah! He was very nice. No, yeah, he asked me to dinner…I know! Anyway I just *had* to let someone know. Yes, enjoy the lake!" She hung up, feeling giddy. Heather Raulston was easily her favorite person to call when she felt like this, nipples perked and heart open. Heather never really seemed to care about her excitedness, leveling Hannah out enough to stave off her crazy. Well, sort of.

33.

State street stood busily awake in the mid hours of the afternoon. Cabs were heiled, the buzz was about--it was almost happy hour! Most socialites walked briskly and drank about, not really caring nor understanding what the two deaths meant. Well, the two they knew about. The murders even took place on the bad side of town. Typical.

The firetrucks whirred by and flung themselves down State, vaulting ahead of the kerfuffle. No one really noted them, save for the annoyance of the siren. They heard it but it was just a firetruck. No one fusses over a fire truck. Dogs do, cats maybe.

We find our heroes ahead of the trucks, already trying to put out a fire in a warehouse.

"So how did this work again?" Rye asked Hitch. Birdie was along with them, too. Salem was back home with the cats, so to speak.

"Well," Hitch said, "I boosted the hose mechanism from a fire truck so that we could use hydrants instead of having to lug around that barrel of water. Birdie!"

"Yeah," Birdie was inside the warehouse. The blaze hadn't really made it all the way inward. "He's not in here."

"You sure?"

"Yeah."

"Shit."

"Yeah."

"Alright," Hitch said, "Rye?"

"Wrap it up?"

"Ayuh."

The gang got their things and sauntered out. They sped off on their dirt bikes, leaving the building mostly still afire as the trucks pulled up.

34.

It made sense to Him, them coming to the warehouse; they were self-glorified heroes, afterall. Marcus didn't appear to be with them, duh, He cackled, Marcus was there on the forest floor, and would rot if He left the kid. It was almost a nice sight to Him, seeing them bound across an empty field while smoke billowed about and the sun shined, heroic work to be done. Soon they were blotted out there on the other end, where the field met the forest-line, they disappeared. He spat, picked Marcus up, wandered off, holding himself together, tho barely.

He had an idea.

35.

It was late, Ben stretching and cursing, rubbing his head, hoping to come up with just a bit more. The cursor blinked before him. The power had gone out hours ago and his laptop was on its last juice. He stared some more at the screen and decided his cleverness had found its limit. He thought he heard some ruckus and assumed it was Heather and Hector going at it again. He grabbed a flashlight and went to find his way out of the maze that was Hank's west wing. When he finally found the living room everyone was on the floor, unconscious. Hitch was lying there like he'd been knocked in the head. But where was Hank? He looked around as the lightning gave him a bit more sight and there he was being dragged by

"Marcus?"

Marcus looked up at him but he was not Marcus at all. Ben wanted to vomit.

"Guess again," said the figure. It was Him. He cocked His head to the side and Ben could see His grin from underneath Marcus' face. "Ya know," He said, "a face is actually pretty easy to skin off. Once the blood dried it practically stuck to my face on its own."

Ben readied himself but was still in total disbelief and shock as He closed the space the between them. He knew Ben was scared beyond his wits so He took His time. Reaching behind Himself, it looked like He might produce a samurai sword but when Ben was hit it wasn't with a blade, rather a cold, dead arm.

Ben was slapped, repeatedly, in the face with the arm and hand, eventually it knocked the flashlight to the floor, wriggled its way around his neck, like a muscular piano wire.

Then he was being dragged. Then out.

145

"Why would they do that?" He asked, hair flailing wildly in the night wind, eyes like tar. "C'mon, why?" He asked again, slapping an unresponsive man with what looked to be another man's severed arm. "I mean hold up camp in a house I not only know exists, but can easily break into?" He put the arm out of his window, allowing the wind to flap it around. "you know, Ben" He said, "you lot aren't too smart." There was a face superglued to his own, like a horrible, stench-ridden, mask. "They'll come for you, though." He grinned, it was an ugly grin. "It would have been done," he slapped the man again with the arm—more violently this time—and yelled, angrily, "but no! You had to walk out of nowhere! HOW AM I SUPPOSED TO KILL *YOU*?? FUCK!!! I DIDN'T THINK *YOU'D* JOIN UP! STUPID SONOFABITCH!!!" He was violently inconsolable, weaving in and out of lanes, almost went up on a curb in attempt to hit a pedestrian.

In his rage he didn't see the sport utility vehicle pull up beside him.

"Hey pal," said the muzzle of a twelve-gauge.

He looked over and saw it pointed at His open window.

"You messed with the wrong motherfuckers, limp dick."

He hit his breaks, dumped the body, and sped off in the direction he had come from. The SUV pulled up, grabbed Salem, and sped around towards His vehicle.

Salem started coming to. The man who had the gun was up front in the passenger seat and slapped his face a bit, only with his own hand.

"Alright, alright," Salem said. "I'm up." He looked around in attempt to familiarize himself with where he was and why.

"Relax," said the guy with the shotgun. He was a handsome fellow who looked to have ancestors hailing from the middle-east. "We'll get the motherfucker." He cocked his gun.

"How did you?"

"Man I know who Hector is and I know when my friends are in trouble. We've been keeping an eye."

"But the guns," Salem said.

The man who was driving was a large black man and he gave a hearty laugh.

"You guys knew I had these, what'd you think they were for?"

"Tell 'um," the driver said.

"Now arm yourself," he said, cocking a nine-millimeter and putting it to Salem's palm, "and Ben?"

"Yeah Seem?"

"Don't think I forgot about that quarter you wanted a front on. You're about to see what my drug pushing, gun cocking, ruthless-ass self is capable of." He grinned, winked, and then stuck his gun out of the window.

Salem looked out and watched the SUV catch up to the side of the compact, and the man who nabbed him. Salem opened his window and went about to aim. The rain began to beat down again.

"Ninety-five!" The driver yelled, "OHHHHHH BABY!"

The two cars sped neck to neck down State. The cops must have been off eating doughnuts or something.

Salem jumped from his window and into the rain. He was lucky enough to be wearing his belt, though no mask. He pulled out a claw that dug into the roof of the vehicle. Were it not raining Salem could have managed without the claw. He laid on top of the car, the SUV next to him, his friends too busy cheering him on to do any kind of helping. That is when Salem saw the bridge and felt the vehicle beneath him veer towards it. He shot, pop pop, frantically into the roof under him, hoping to hit something, anything. He did, but only a leg. The bridge was upon them, Ben knew this nut job was going to run both cars off. When the two vehicles were airborne only seconds held between them and the water. It must have been thirty, forty feet. Salem jumped from the top of the car up towards the heavens before dive bombing in and after Haseem's SUV. When he hit the water he stroked furiously for it. As he approached he could hear a song vibrating through the water and scaring the fish. It was eerie because it was all he could hear, the blurring of droned out base and the overwhelming sound of an all too familiar voice

I got

niggas

in the head piece

who know right where

your girl

be resting.

So give me that

Mutha

(Mutha)

Fuckin'

(Fuckin')

Money

The headlights of Haseem's SUV were still on, tho fading, clinging to life while short circuiting, pointing down into a dark, underwater, void.

He got to the window, it was open and Haseem was inside struggling with his safety belt. His compatriot had a piece of the bridge through his skull. The headlights flickered off and the song died. Salem's lungs screamed for oxygen. There were protests amongst his cells for it, 'LEAVE HIM!! GET AIR!!' they screamed. He flicked out a knife and felt for the belt.

He found it, gave it a flick of his wrist.

They both swam back towards the surface and out of the river. Haseem passed out as soon as land was met and he was bleeding. Salem looked about, desperately searching for an idea. He looked from the basketball courts to the fields for anyone who might help him. He saw an old blue Foard off in the park they washed up on, and went over to it, hoping the gods would be kind to him. They smiled brightly. No one was in it, he'd saved one of his keys when he traded his own old blue Foard in, ultimately for an occasion such as this. A chance. It clicked over, bid him entrance. The engine puttered to a roar when he found the ignition.

He pulled around and grabbed Haseem, speeding the few some-odd blocks to Hitch's. Once there, he pulled in and grabbed Haseem from the back. When he turned around Hitch was already in front him, offering help. They carried Haseem up the stairs and into Hitch's, which already seemed to be some kind of makeshift hospital, plenty of gauze, cots strewn about.

"Fuck," Rye said, "you guys look like shit."

"Said the pot," Haseem coughed up.

Rye got up to help Haseem to the couch and everyone asked where they had come from and how Haseem had gotten involved. Salem told the tale without embellishment.

"So you jumped off the top of a car as it flung through the air towards the river."

"Yeah."

"I don't believe it." Rye said. He and Salem had found their way to the kitchen and were drinking along with twiddling their thumbs. "Who'd have thought our drug dealer would be the one to step in and help us out?"

"I didn't see it coming."

"Well, you were knocked out."

Salem took the pull that finished his glass off and stared into the emptiness of it.

"Another, Sir?"

"Jesus, Butler," Rye half-jumped, "don't sneak up on us like that." Rye drained his glass, "make that two."

"So you're all just going to sit here playing doctors and drunks, then?" The old man asked, pouring the drinks.

"This stopped being a game awhile ago, Butler."

150

"Spoken like a writer. A wordsmith does have to keep his whittle to the grindstone, I suppose."

"And what about you, Butler? Go turn some beds over or dust something. Lots of fucking good you do."

"Don't take it out on him." Rye chirped in. "You're just mad because he's right."

"Whatever, I'm still not sure what he's doing here."

"Would you have me alone in a house with a psychopath?"

"Would you have me admit that I don't give a fuck?"

"Sir," said Butler, "you are a noble man with a quick-wit. Tell me," he said, "how many men might jump on not only one, but two cars, in the rain, with one of them moments from crashing into the abyss?"

"It was a river," Rye said, "tone it down."

Salem took another drink. He didn't answer.

"Well," Butler said, "I suppose I should be off, beds to turn over and all."

Salem chuckled behind his closed mouth. "Hey," he said, Butler paused, "are you one of those men?"

"No, sir." And he was off.

Hitch's kitchen was no more than a fridge, a — very — small bar, and a two burner stove bought at a camping supply depot.

"What do you think it's like?" Rye asked.

"What?"

"Dying."

"I don't think it's like anything. You know, when you do come to the moment of death you just trip balls."

"Yeah, the DMT. Everyone knows."

"Exactly. So one minute you're walking down the street and then your brain blasts off, and that's all you ever know before the lights go out."

"What if they don't go out?" Rye asked. "Time is relative, so how long would that trip last, an eternity?"

"No," Salem said. "We all go. Do you think Marcus is still hallucinating?"

"I suppose not. What about your soul?"

"You're asking the wrong guy, pal. I believe in organs shutting down and electrodes being turned off and shit. When it's over there won't be anything. No memory, no nothing. Might as well be a rock."

"Jesus." Rye sat for a moment and twirled his drink, basking in every emotion he'd ever felt. "You think they'll forget us?"

Salem was surprised at Hank's frankness, normally he didn't ponder anything for too long. "Before all of this I would have said yes but now, now I'm not so sure. Taking down a once in a generation maniac, all dressed as batman. No, I don't think we'll be easily forgotten."

"He wouldn't be here if we weren't--the maniac."

"I know what you mean there, Faulkner. Maybe we should all just jump from a bridge then. But, maybe he's not after us." Rye took a pull and had a look of seriousness about him for the first time in many moons. "He's out to oust the light with the dark." They both thought a moment, the groans from the other room piercing the ears they held. "Is that why you write?"

"What?"

"To oust the dark?"

"No, I just don't know what else to do."

"You might try writing a sentence that means a damn."

Salem laughed. "Even when I do well people only want to like what they think they see in themselves. And no one wants to know how fucking stupid he is."

"Yeah," Rye poured another drink, "this whiskey does taste good with this ginger."

"Yeah," Salem lit up a cigarette. "So what do we do?"

"We stop him. We have to."

"How?"

"How would you do it?"

The sun was coming up on a new day.

38.

"You couldn't have taken a load for free?"

Asher Chase pulled out his money clip and flipped through a few bills. The alleyway seemed much more like bile than it had before he came, it seemed rank, and he felt like a freshly cut onion for having his monkey betwixt the lips of a thick Latina whore. He had to be the hundredth monkey that day. Her mouth felt tired. He wondered how strong her jowls must be, probably as rock hard and forceful as his own abs.

"What time do you usually start?"

"Ten pm." She said, wiping herself off with a dumpster rag. Her breasts were as large as her vaginal canal. "Why?"

"I was just thinking at that time your mouth would be…"

"Not worn?"

"Yeah. It must be…"

"Tighter?"

"Yeah."

"It is; you know I've never thought about that before. I have the mouth of a pit bull and the tongue of a snake. You look like you might be ready for round two." She made herself look like she would enjoy another cock in her mouth.

"While I do thank you for your cervix, I must be off." Asher pulled a smoke from her bra strap and lit it, leaving the alleyway behind him.

After a few steps, the streetlights around him began to go out the more he walked. Asher chuckled to himself, "always with the grand entrances." They shut off in pairs, down the street.

The sun would be up soon-ish but for now it was still fairly dark.

"Shut the fuck up, Asher. Where are they?"

"No foreplay today? Damn shame."

He thought he saw a shadow move and sure enough he had. That was always the first thing he'd see during these little visits, a forgotten blur too far adrift in his peripherals to be considered noticeable. There were no cars scurrying by, there were no one save for the whores a few blocks to his back.

"I will pull that fucker right off, Asher." Laughter, "foreplay. Where are they."

"I don't know."

"BULLSHIT!" A fist came hurling and hit Asher in the stomach. His physical stature could take quite the punch, but this felt like a tank had grown fists to shell him.

His eyes opened up right in front of Asher's face: the white of them almost enough to freeze Asher where he stood.

"Do what you will. The only thing I can tell you is that I know absolutely nothing about the old one. I'd wager to say he's got a spot or two worth hiding in."

"They are not hiding!"

Asher laughed, of course they weren't hiding, recovering maybe, but not hiding. He kept them close and knew enough to keep his private life far from those who crusaded the night. Had they found out Asher's hobbies he wouldn't know until he'd slip into some apartment some night and be greeted by Rye, Hitch, Salem, and Birdie. And god damned did they fight dirty. "I told you what underestimating them would do."

"Please, they are running in fear!" When He spoke He seemed to start in at a normal tone and with each word work his way up to a violent yell, not unlike a caveman. "Why are you laughing?!"

"You're delusional. You still think you're coming out of all this, don't you?"

"Why wouldn't I?" He looked at Asher like the handsome little prick was insane; His voice was suddenly more docile. "Do you not believe I can do it?"

"You just don't get it. You're not the one to be feared in this little scenario."

"I don't like the things you're saying!" He slammed another fist in to Asher.

"Okay, Okay." Asher still had a grin on his face despite the blood dripping from his pie hole. "Look, this is something that is beneficial to both our wants, remember, same team and all that jabber jabber. Give me some time to look into it. I really have no fucking idea where they are but I know the places to look."

He smiled at Asher, "was that so hard?"

Asher was glad when He was gone; He smelled like He'd been rooting around in spoiled eggs, and probably had been. "You've got some issues you need to sort through!" Asher yelled out into the darkness. Maybe being on His side was not the smart choice. Asher tried shaking His confidence but it was of no use, He was the one to fear, and Asher may soon be rendered useless in His mentally ill and incapable mind.

Dawn was due to break, Asher had to be on television. Hopefully everyone would be watching.

39.

Ba-back on the map

back in the

back of a bad bitch's

neck.

All outta cash/

check?

Naw, check this/ if I go

aint no one else praying for kendrick/im wreckless,

effectively in tune with the

collective

UH

Get this monkey off my

back

when my mac

(brak-brak-brak)

get disruptive

when you silly little

field niggas

start to plant

gardens/ Oh my lord when

I get rich and

on to Foarbe's list

ya'll be nautious

all the raunchy

shit be-

gotten by my money

(0000-0000)

Young Theo sat with speakers, various tools, what appeared to be a sex swing, and the stink of emotional disability and fear and that pride which makes men quiet as things get worse. It was too much. What was he to do but sit around and rot? Every time he ventured to think his world would implode all over again. No words could reach his core, but Marcus did try, posthumously.

The stainless steel cabinets vibrated along with the speakers. Theo couldn't have the music up loud enough. It drowned his thoughts, made Marcus real again.

What the fuck was going on, anyway?

Last Theo heard that Ben guy—who always wandered off when shit was going down—had jumped from the top of one car to another as both both lept from a bridge. Not only did he save *a* drugdealer, he saved *his* drugdealer. Though when Theo had called him one he said he didn't like the word and explained how he didn't sell drugs because his were natural. He did sell coke though, Theo knew Haseem. Theo knew every single one of the merry band of faggots who were protecting him.

The only thing holding him in place was fear, and he was rooted in it.

He welcomed the cool, dark, tool-laden room Hitch had named Theo's sanctuary: only Theo in or out. Hitch seemed to understand Theo's want for isolation, in his absolute need to forget who people were for a while. He'd simply get lost in his music and think about what his life still may be; it could just get worse from here, it could get better, the chances of both were about the same. But, men often bet on the state of the horse rather than the odds--well a good one will bet on both--by the strut, and the confidence with which a mare could both shit and walk.

Theo was perhaps too many years or too many tragedies from seeing how big a role he needed to play in his own destiny.

Why play the odds when you can make them?

Theo's brain had had too much, red-lining consciousess both sub and fore could take its own toll.

I just know that things

feel better

when I'm bustin'

this berretta.

Cuz when I aim

it's to bang

a spot

in your left

ventricle.

got my homies

try to roll me

stick all on ya

stack your friends up

with your momma

like lasagna

Fuck.

Ain't no sense in guessin'/I'm the best/ here's the evidence/Eminem synonyms, flailing confetti because I'm impudent—sorry hoe—Crawling like a turtle with the city on my back, matta fact/grab a map/I'll take any little city where the hoes is getting busy and the trees is really spiffy/get a spliffy role it up/got a dubee? Role it up/you got speakers? Turn it up/pop the trunk/ Fuck

"Theo," Heather Raulston's smooth voice cut through the music like butter through pie. She shut the door behind her. Theo gave her a once over. "Hitch said it was alright, that I.."

"…come in here?" Theo asked.

"Yeah."

"Alright. Just close the door behind you."

Heather turned around, confused. She looked at the door, already closed, then at Theo, then back again.

"I'm fucking with you, sit down."

Heather sat next to Theo and was quiet. The music kicked and she looked around at what was quite the curious room: weird tools, mad-scientist-like mash-ups of weapons with other weapons. Theo heard the quiver of her lip and the breaking of her dam. He slipped his arm around her and let her bare all. Yes, she cried. Tho, if storms pass we can assume everything else does, too, right?

"Hank wants us to leave. He bought train tickets to his cottage in Bangor. Says he'll give us enough money to start over, let you grow up."

"What are they going to be doing?"

"Hunting, I suppose. They said they'd be sleeping in the sewers until that shmuck is dead. Hitch also suggested that we stay, help. Someone to communicate maybe, Hitch has some computers downstairs, police scanners, all kinds of cool shit."

"Do you want to go?"

"No, but you should, Butler said he'd take care of you, and I'm still not 100% sure I won't go."

"I don't know."

"Well, they're leaving tonight. So would we. Think on it."

Theo put his head back and breathed. The sun was making itself fully known and all Theo wanted was sleep. He wanted to get the sonofabitch who'd slain his mother but really he was not up to it. What could he offer? He wasn't even a teen yet. He was scared too, but not of Him. He was scared of not having the skills necessary to make anything possible. He'd like to see himself at the end, victorious, but it just wasn't feasible. Where was his slick mouth and confidence now? He was no horse to hastily bet on. He was a kid who feared he had over-estimated himself. He could be comfortable. He could not rise up now, or ever, and be blissfully happy as he would shove everything behind him and use a routine to numb anything genuine that he had within himself. Failure. It hung over him like the knife that would ultimately come down if he did fail. Even if he succeeded it wouldn't bring anyone back, and if these past few days had taught him anything—and they had—he'd just be asked to do it again and again and again. Did he have the grapes? Did he even care to have them?

"Don't put what you want to do on me." He spoke up.

"What?" Heather really couldn't hear him through the music. Theo shut it off.

"Don't put your future on me."

"I just..."

"I know. And I appreciate you for it, but if you want to stay or if you want to go then do it. Don't make me the one who has to decide."

"But you do still have to make a decision."

"I will." Theo's face hardened and he looked too old for the short-pants he was wearing. Heather went to embrace him but Theo would have none of it. "There's fault on both sides."

"But which one is the right side?"

"Bitch, I don't know. I'm twelve."

Heather smiled. "I was being rhetorical, dingus."

"Yeah, twelve year-olds know what rhetoric is."

"You do."

Theo sat and knew he was being stubborn. "Fuck, Heather. I don't know. How can you guys even expect me to do this?"

"We don't"

"Then why ask?"

"Hitch thought..."

"I know, I know that I might like taking part in bringing Him to justice. But what does it matter who serves it up?"

"I don't know. That's up to you." She kissed him on the head and left him alone.

Theo sat up and walked the room. It was marvelous. There were spare black suits of various sizes and actual weapons that could maim: an electrified knife, a slingshot with pellet sized explosives, bows and arrows which would separate into more arrows when shot, tomahawks, swords, gelatin blobs that would stick and explode. Even the shit that could not maim was cool. There were grappling hooks, drones, a single jetpack, gliding suits, and many many other things; all of which he had his pick of.

He found an odd little headpiece and put it on. It made a noise and in the corner a tiny blue light blinked and one of the drones whirred up and flew over behind him. He stood there for a moment as it hovered, wahwahwahwah.

"Play some music." He said out loud.

Jalapeno genome.

Bitch,

I'm hot.

"Stop." The music stopped. "It's dark in here."

Would you like some light? The voice came from within his head and it sounded like his mother's. He forced his hand to his open mouth as his entire face stung with hot sadness, like somehow blocking his air intake could stop his tear ducts from doing what they do best.

"I would love some," he finally managed to let out. A soft light came from the drone and illuminated the room.

Is that better?

"Much."

Theo found a black suit to match his size and adorned it, this motherfucker would be one burnt-ass piece of toast. Walking around with his hair long and unwashed, wearing body paint like some kind of faggot. He found a few explosives and a crossbow and some other hair-brained mechanisms and went in front of the mirror at the far end of the room, his drone buzzing behind him.

You look formidable

He grinned because he felt that way in his uniform with his weapons. His belly burned with passion and commitment. He opened the door from the laboratory and smelled pot smoke coming from the room to his left, the room everyone else was in. He heard laughter, though it was pained. He snuck passed the room and out of Hitch's door. The day was bright and warm. His decension was quick. Stairs conquered, Theo shot a glance back at the house. Unlike those who talked of doing something, Theo was about to roam the streets himself and stop wasting time with plans or shittalking.

He made way towards State. He'd start down on Destin, where he'd find his mother's former employees. They'd have to know something.   Any information would be good information.   Someone had to be talking somewhere, this lunatic didn't get his information on gut instinct alone.

Destin had a few whores scurrying about but he went with familiarity when he walked up to Shaneesha.

"Hey," he said in a voice outside of his own. His drone had gone up over the buildings per his request.

"Hey yourself. Any weird shit is double."

"I'm not looking for weird shit."

"That little outfit says otherwise."

"Shut the fuck up." Theo stood with sunglasses over his mask so his eyes might be masked. He looked strange. "You heard about Marcus?"

"Yeah, him and that DJ of his still owe me money."

"I don't care about that."

"Then I don't care to participate in whatever the fuck this is."

Theo handed her a few crisp hundreds--he'd found them stuffed in a nice money tree Hank had in his parlor. He'd probably found upwards of twenty thousand dollars holed up in that house. He'd kept it in his backpack but transferred it to a blackpack he'd found in Hitch's secret room.

"I'm listening." Shaneesha said.

"You been telling anyone about my cohorts?"

Shaneesha knew his uniform. "Out in broad daylight today? You guys must be getting desperate."

"Who was around here the night she died?"

"A lot of people."

"Who have ties with us?"

"Well, George Hammer. Asher Chase."

Theo knew Mr. Hammer was skeez just from how Hitch had described him but he was all about the money. Asher was interesting. He was upstanding, clean, and the rest of the gang seemed to meet with him often. "Asher?"

"Yeah, he was here this morning too. He comes around. I thought you guys knew tho."

"So?"

"So…"

"The beans, woman, spill them."

"That's all."

"Who was he with this morning?"

Shaneesha pointed to the latina. Theo walked over to her and gave her cash before the two exchanged any words.

"This kind of money means some weird shit. Did you at least clean the asshole I'm about to lick? And I don't mean just a wipe."

"That's not what I'm here for." Theo felt larger than himself.

"Oh, good."

"Asher Chase."

"Who?"

Theo paused and looked through his sunglasses at her. She knew what he'd meant and people who played dumb made him furious.

"Look he has me suck his dick a lot. I don't know what you'd want with him. Fuck, you guys are down here talking to him all the time."

"Shut up."

"Everybody knows."

"He seems a bit upstanding to be down here, no?"

She laughed. "Images can be just that sometimes. He comes around here more than I do."

So Asher was scum. "He's probably just looking for a scoop."

"Yeah, on you guys."

"What?"

I can't count how many times he's asked me and Shaneesha over there about when you come here, why, who you see."

"And you just give what he wants?"

"Sweetie," she said, rolling her eyes, looking at the money Theo just handed her, "please."

"Does he ever meet anyone else?"

"Lots of people, usually just in a professional manner though, shooting whatever shit can be shot to hide himself."

"What about this morning?"

"What's to tell? He came in my mouth and then left."

"To where?"

"His job."

Theo thanked her and left. He had direction and purpose.

He knows something. The voice from his drone sounded just as close as it had in close quarters. Theo could hear his little machine hovering up above, his heart was oddly calm and the fog that had hung in his brain was clearing.

He made his way over to NewsNet Two as quickly as he could, remaining conscious of staying in cover. He still had to be careful. The man who killed his mother was still out and around and looking for someone who'd be dressed just as Theo was. He stuck out like an erection in silk pants. He should have brought a change of clothes. The day was too bright for him to be bumbling around in something so identifiable. The pavement in the alleyways he cut down was hard and hot. The buildings loomed over him and he began to feel small again. What kind of idiot would run around wearing this costume right now?

You are hunting this man. Not the other way around.

167

For a machine the drone sure knew what the fuck it was talking about. Theo went out in hopes of finding his mother's killer, butt he'd settle for that psychopath finding him. Whatever it took to wring His neck.

He arrived at the news station with ease and snuck through a back door as he took his mask off, leaving the rest of his uniform intact. He went around and approached the front desk, his small brown face did not show the shakiness within him.

"How may I help you?" The desk clerk was a plump woman who looked at him curiously. It was the response Theo was looking for.

"Hi, I'm here to see Asher Chase. I've been wearing this costume for days and I wanted to go on television to show my support for the good in this town."

She smiled and looked like she might shed a tear or two. "Do you have an appointment?"

Theo looked at his shoes. "No."

"Well let me see..." She typed a bit on her computer and her chin wobbled along with her fingers. "His schedule is clear for the next few hours. He's on air right now but you can wait in his office if you'd like."

He looked up at her and smiled. "Thank you so much."

"Can I have your name for our logs?"

"Yes, Marcus Vance."

"Alright, Marcus, one moment."

She grabbed her phone and said a few words and a moment later a nice looking soon-to-be woman came around the corner. Her shirt was a bit low if professionalism is what she was going for, but she still looked damned good and with how much care she seemed to take of her body no one would be the asshole to tell her to cover up a bit. The woman at the desk looked at her like she might've looked that way once herself. Time and squeezing out kids and menopause had turned her into what she was. So too would it be for that perky bitch one day, almost cursing her.

"Marcus?" The girl looked at him and smiled, her teeth were chiseled ivory. Marcus was right in the middle of realizing how arousing females could be and noticed only that she could probably gargle a nice dick.

"Yes." He said.

"Come with me." She led him down a corridor and past the office that said, in big letters, 'Asher Chase'. "I'm not supposed to do this but I'm going to give you a peek into the studio. Just be quiet. Asher, I mean Mr. Chase, is on air right now." Theo noticed her cheeks redden.

When they stepped into the studio no one made a move to look back at where Theo stood. It was not at all what he was expecting. He'd imagined a great room with lights everywhere and high ceilings and a window behind the anchors set to show the backdrop of his city. Instead he walked in to a small and dank room with a picture behind Asher of some view off State. The place reeked of cigarettes and everyone smelled like bologna that was left in the son a bit too long. The lights were there, but they were few. Asher sat behind a desk by his lonesome. A few lights were on him and he looked like a man who feared for his life:

"....and I can't do it anymore, frankly. Do you know who Hector Bridge is? He is one of the vigilantes, I have spoken with him on many occasions. If what's going to stop this madman is turning these thugs in then we do it with zest. I do

169

it with zest. Another member is Hank Green, the toilet paper billionaire….."

The girl hurried Theo out and down towards Asher's office. "It's just horrible what is happening out there. I don't see why anyone else has to suffer just for those men you are supporting."

"You really think He'd stop at just them?"

"Yes, I do." She opened the door to the office and Theo plopped on the couch. She did not enter with him and closed the door as she walked away.

40

Theo looked around and about at the esteemed journalist's shit. His office was void of any pictures with family or friends. Theo stood up from the couch and ran his hand along the large oaken desk across the room. It was a tiny room, had one window. The desk, a few this and that's on it and there was a bookcase with some older Stephen King novels.

Theo checked the door for a lock and found it, he pushed in the tiny little nub and went back behind Asher's desk, opening the drawers: filled with nonsense and random scribbling on pieces of paper. Theo continued rummaging and found a rough sketch on a random piece of printing paper. It was of the man who'd killed his mother, the man who'd killed Marcus. He looked at it for a second longer and then was jolted back from whatever trance he'd been in. The handle on the door had jiggled and now it was flailing wildly, like whomever was outside might break the damned thing down just to get in. Then, it subsided and all was quiet. Theo slid the sketch back to its home and carefully slid the drawer closed, as quietly as he could.

Knock Knock

Theo kept calm, his big brown eyes gathered in everything: exit strategies, weapons, possible conversation pattern, the sprinklers up overhead. It is what hid on the floor under Asher's desk which caught the boy's eye. He wanted to bend down and examine it but he hadn't the time.

Knock Knock

The knocks were now growing impatient. Theo went to the door and opened it. Asher stood there and cocked his head to the side, looking the tiny man up and down.

"Asher Chase!" Theo made his best to sound star struck.

Asher stood outside of the door and continued looking at Theo. "Theo Mathis," Asher said, "why did you tell my assistant you were Marcus Slaughter?"

"What?"

"I came in here expecting to see a ghost. You here because I gave them up?"

"It was a stunt. Tells me you're hiding something. Besides, their names won't matter, they'll still be hiding away in their little hole. I'm here because I have questions."

The boy was a bit paranoid and in his thoughts Asher was already guilty of something, and what were those black paint drippings under that desk over there?

Asher entered and quickly closed the door behind him. Theo saw something in the back of his eyes, it might have been worry, it might have been remorse. "I came to see what you really know." Theo replied. "Those cocksuckers at Hitch's won't tell me shit."

"Oh, they're at Hitch's?" Asher asked.

Theo looked at him: what an odd question. Theo felt stupid for slipping up that kind of information, but was perplexed at Asher's inquiry into their whereabouts. Theo could see Asher struggling with trying to appear vaguely curious, something back in Theo's mind knew the man was burning to know where Rye and them were. Theo laughed, "of course, man. Where else would they be?"

Asher laughed, uneasily, "I don't know. Anyway, you've been closer to this whole thing then I have, shouldn't you know what is going on? I've been living on the morsels of peanut crumbs from Hitch."

"They're keeping this one close, Asher, you can understand."

After milling around his office for a minute, pacing between the small office walls like mouse in a cracker box, he went to speak but could not. He was looking for something from Theo, an 'in'. Theo could sense it.

"So what are you," Asher began, his pace finding its way to the mini bar and the crystalline rocks glasses fit upon it, "a messenger boy?" Asher flashed himself a smile and fixed a drink. He poured some iced tea for Theo.

The bustle of the media station rumbled on outside of Asher's closed door. Theo could hear shouting from editors to producers and then the various cameramen arguing over which anchoress they might like to stick their sweaty, pinky sized, pricks in to. Phones rang and were answered importantly; every call could be the next nine eleven.

"So you knew my mom?" Theo began.

"What?" Asher was taken by the hairs on his neck.

"Yeah," Theo took the glass of iced tea from Asher and took a sip, "you were always down by her whores. Someone likes to get sucked off before the sun comes up."

Asher took a sip of his drink and looked down at Theo. He was thinking on what a strange child this one had turned out to be. His mom had died; Asher couldn't exactly blame the kid for going nuts. His language, his demeanor, stank of a being older than his thirteen or so years. "Why are you here, Theo?"

Theo grinned. He had all he'd came for. "Whose side are you on, Asher?"

The handsome man standing before Theo downed the rest of his drink in one large gulp. His face lit up and roasted from the fire in his belly. He poured some more of the brown liquid and took another swig. "Did you see the end of that telecast?"

173

Theo had not so he said, "no."

Asher flicked on his television and said, "watch." The television by the couch looked quite new, Asher flipped to the files the audio visual device might have access to. "What the hell," he said. "There's only one file in here."

"Play it." Theo said, as though he had a loaded gun to Asher's face.

He did. The video started in without a fade and before both Asher and Theo was a dark bedroom. Asher recognized the room instantly; it was dark when he'd entered it only hours before. He caught himself from saying 'Hannah' out loud as he watched her sleep there in her bed. Whomever was filming was doing so from the closet, it appeared. In the camera frame was her bed, mirror, most of a wall.

"What the fuck is this." Theo said, not asking a question so much as demanding an answer.

Asher looked at him in bewilderment, he knew the setting and the girl but he did not know who was filming; his confusion was true, so Theo could not see through it.

The video played for another five minutes and nothing happened besides the occasional snore from the woman occupying the bed. She didn't move once as she slept. Theo looked, wondering what might happen.

A light, a light flickered on from somewhere and then off. The camera angle was only broad enough to catch a glimpse of the handle on the door, and the far corner of the bedroom. It was small.

The handle to the door turned; Theo glanced over at Asher; he look unsettled, disquieted. The bedroom was very dark, Theo brought his eyes back to Asher's television and saw a man, or a figure at the very least, slink into the room with the sleeping girl. Theo watched and became certain it was a broad shouldered man and that that man was staring down and touching the girl. Flashes went off and Theo realized it was a camera. The entire scene was bizarre. But still, who was filming this?

It was all but certain, the figure roaming in the girl's room was a man. He could be seen rummaging through a few drawers, picking panties at his leisure, sniffing them. Eventually he made his way back to the bed, standing over the girl sleeping just there and almost touching her hair before exiting, almost hypnotized.

Asher was paler than a ginger kid on a cold January afternoon. He was sweating, and he appeared to be sick. "What is this?" He asked.

Theo didn't think Asher was addressing him. Once the girl's room quieted down again, say three minutes later, the camera moved slowly from out of the closet, right next to the bed. The girl lying there did not stir, even with the camera nearly on her face, it turned and zoomed and lingered. Whoever was holding the thing even got into bed with her. Her body was more on the thick side of things but she even slept like she might like to have a cock in between the great tits hanging from her.

Theo remained quiet and watched. He saw an arm, a great black arm, go over her like he might have been comforting her. The camera began to swing around and the room whirled and turned. When it settled it was facing back on the sleeping beauty, towards where the closet was, but she was the only one in the picture. Where did the arm go?

She lied there, peacefully, for an entire minute that felt like an eon. Theo squirmed, Asher stared and stared. His office entombed them and felt so ancient that it was almost nonexistent. "Hi Asher." A voice rang out, sinister and distant. The girl opened her eyes and saw the camera and looked at it like she might a just-crashed flying saucer. She tilted her head this way and then that, the darkness behind her palpable. His face popped up behind her, black and covered with hair. It peeked up from right above her shoulder as she sat there staring at the camera like a moron. He ran the ends of his tangled up hair on her delicate shoulder and she froze up. Her face looked stone hard, like she'd already went through rigor mortis.

She reached up and grabbed the hair on her shoulder and turned around to scream, the video cut out.

41

Theo stared at the blank screen of the television for a moment and then at Asher. He was still staring.

"I don't know, Asher," Theo said, "*what was that*?" The insinuation in his tone was heavy.

"I don't know."

"Do you know her?" Theo asked.

"No."

"Then who is she?"

"I don't know."

Asher was sweating like a clam who'd just finished a triathlon. His eyes were shifty and he was up from the couch and pacing like a lunatic. He kept mouthing 'what the fuck what the fuck fuck fuck' even though nothing blew through his vocal chords.

"Asher?"

"What?"

"What's wrong?"

"What the fuck do you think is wrong, kid? This mother fucker has dragged me in to all of this and is now apparently just killing random people in my name."

"Did you know my mom?" Theo asked. He already knew the answer, but that's the only way someone can tell a liar, to ask a question that already had an answer.

"Yes." Asher said, "she was a lovely woman. But I'm not the reason she's dead, Birdie is."

"How did you know that?" Asher's asshole had noticeably puckered up. "Asher," Theo said, "how did you know that?"

The handsome and cool of Asher had all left him, he was now a worm in dry earth squirming in hopes it might bring rain. He was different, he was fidgety, and his sentences were uneven, left off without punctuation.

"I…I mean…look…most…most people…"

"How was that blowjob this morning?"

"What?"

"How was it?" Theo was right there. What was this hump he couldn't get over? Where were the words, the right words? What did he have to say? He knew Asher had a part in all of this, but he didn't know which part. The man was ambiguous at best, nothing about anything made sense; he was clearly not the killer but he was also not innocent. And Theo was just a kid. What could he do right now?

Theo remembered two weeks ago and it were all alright, then. Asher sat next to him, pale-faced. What a sight he was. Theo knew the look in his face: guilt.

"Did you love her, too?" Theo asked.

"What?"

"The girl in the video," Theo said, "Hec loved my mom. Did you love her?"

"In a way," Asher replied, taking pause and thinking on the question. Theo realized his mistake. Asher looked on the young costumed man and tilted his head, about to speak. Asher's sentence was cut off short. A bullet fizzled into the center of his head.

Theo saw the hole in Asher's dome but was confused and ducked and searched around for the origin of the bullet; he was also searching for cover. He sought refuge down by the baseboards, watching blood drip from just due north of Asher's nose.

Theo lay flat and heard no more shots; the life slipped from Asher and on to nirvana. After a few minutes he heard a familiar voice in his head.

What are you doing? The female/robot voice asked

Theo thought about what the drone could mean, he was obviously in distress.

I got rid of him, like you wanted.

What? Theo wondered. The voice from the drone sounded too far into his mind for Theo to be comfortable. It was like the thing had attached itself to his brain and reacted upon his whimsies.

You saw the look in his eyes, and thought he should be shot, so I shot him. You seemed pretty sure about it five seconds ago.

"Fuck," Theo said out loud, "this man and machine thing always has to go wrong." He took off the headpiece that connected his thoughts to the drone. When he did he felt more himself. He hadn't noticed how much the robot had been a part of him until he removed the headwear. He threw the equipment down on to the floor and stomped on it. He looked out of the window and the drone came balling down from the clouds, exploding in midair, parachuting down to the ground in pieces.

Theo realized he had to get out of there, and fast. Luckily enough for him the falling and exploding drone was enough of a distraction. Young black Theo had time and quickness enough to vault down the stairs and crash through the back door, dash off into the alley behind the Mexican grocery store.

42

"If anything he just wanted me to have a good time," she said, "he's sweet, not malicious."

"So…" Hitch said, "that's why he roofied you? So you'd have a good time?"

"It wasn't roofies, asshole, it was molly."

"MDMA, Reuifnol, what's the difference," Hitch laughed, moving up his spectacles.

Hitch and Heather sat around the table that was set in the middle of Hitch's living room; it was round, wisps of lure were oddly scribbled around the outer ring, in pattern. There was a giant hand in the middle of the table: giving the peace sign.

Hector, Habeep, Ben, and Hank had gone ahead to get the bikes from their unit. Heather could ride Marcus'. They hadn't seen Asher's newscast, outing them.

Hitch wandered off into his room, Heather called after him, "I'm getting you some things," Hitch said, "ski mask, what have you."

After minutes he emerged pleasant-faced with a black ski-mask, a gray jogging suit, taser, steel-toed boots. He took off his own Kevlar vest and gave it to her as well. "You can go change in my room. Do you need anything else?"

"Brass knuckles," Heather said, smiling. She was changing right there in the room, damned it all. "I could really kick some ass right now," she said, throwing on the sweatpants, tying up her boots. She knocked on their tip. She went to take her top off and Hitch decided it to be a good time to get her the brass knuckles from the other room. A pair. He came back in as she was zipping up, bunning her hair and slipping it into the mask, putting up the hood. "Swank," she said.

"Swank, I like it." Hitch said, handing her a radio piece. He hit the button on his own. "Gentleman say hello to Swank."

"Hello," said Birdie

"Hello," said Rye

"Hello," said Salem.

"Hi boys," Swank chimed in

"You sound hot," Birdie doubled back.

"Likewise,"

"Where are you guys?"

"Almost to the unit, dropping Habeep off. He said something about not belonging? That he shouldn't be here I guess, I don't know."

"So how are we…"

"Proceeding?"

"Preciously,"

"Salem and I are going to hang back; Rye is going for the kid."

This was code of course, they used it sometimes, in great danger. Birdie were actually going to get the kid, Rye was hanging back, along with Salem. "Alright," Hitch said, then explaining as much to Heather. "We'll be leaving shortly."

Hitch grabbed a shotgun and slung it to his back. "Let's go, we're gonna walk. Stick with me."

Heather followed, Hitch locked up. They began the trek, down a back alley. Of course, 'walk' was code for jog. When they broke the alley a school bus was parked near the library across the street. The sun was going down, everything eerily quiet. No one dared a chance at being outside. Most of them were watching the news when Asher went off, a man over across state saw both the bus and the masked heroes approaching it from his porch, rolled his eyes, went inside to hide. 'That's probably that asshole boy-king. We outta get pitchforks and pillage that fucker's mansion.' Chuckling all the way.

The bus seemed empty which made it all the stranger. "Probably nothing," Swank said, "kids bussed from school for a reading group, maybe?"

"No," Hitch said, seeing Him as they drew nearer, tho still a football field out. The engine on the bus came to life. Hitch ran to the closest car he could find, luckily for him it had a bit of muscle. He grabbed a small rectangle from his side, hit a button, and a metal bar sprang to life. It looked slim enough to fit down and unlock the car but Hitch bashed it through the window.

"What the fuck,"

"C'mon," Hitch shouted to Heather, bending under the dash of the car. The bus began to pull away. The car tried clicking to life, Heather was still stranded in the road. "Heather!" Hitch yelled, in a moment of lapsed discipline. She was still looking at the damned bus, it pulled out of the parking lot and onto a street towards the highway. "Heather!" Hitch finally got through. Heather ran back to the car, Hitch kept tapping the right wires, they were just not catching, *click click click.*

The bus was stopped at a light by the church, a face peeked up in one of the windows, gagged and taped. Then another.

"Jesus," Heather said, watching the light turn green. She jumped, the car behind her roared to life. Heather ran to the passenger door.

"No," Hitch said, "you drive. Honk twice and then open the trunk when you're in front of the bus. It just went south on the highway."

Heather grabbed the keys and Hitch plunked himself in the trunk. Heather saw holes in the plan but they had little time to deliberate. She had to catch the bus before it ran into the 480, which was only three miles south and ran both east, west. If she didn't at least see where the bus went it would be a fifty fifty shot at guessing which highway to traverse. She gunned it. She could hear Hitch in the trunk trying to reach the others via his radio. She tried too but it was no good. They started yelling to each other about the gameplan once they caught the bus. All green lights, roaring engine, she shook under streetlights like a one-car train. She saw the bus heading south on the bridge above, having just come from the on ramp. A red light hit. She waited, watching the bus get away. Hitch pounded and pounded on the trunk. She realized the red light meant little in this sleepy town, pedaled down, hit the ramp and flipped up to third, then fourth gear, she came around the corner and hit the highway, going from fourth down to third for a spell, the car roared forward and Heather slammed the transmission in the fourth gear then on up to fifth. She misjusdged the distance of the other highway. The school bus was already making its way on that ramp, turning from south to east. The east freeway was more or less devoid of lights. At least she could catch them.

43

Hank had left Habeep on the side of the road. Habeep wanted to be dropped off at home--claiming only that 'he had no idea why he'd involved himself in the first place,'--but Hank had not the time for such things. They were on a wooded road, after some miles there was a turnoff for a park. Hank, Bird and Salem put on their masks and a few more things, some rope etc, ditched the ride, and vaunted into the woods. Headed west down the shoreline of the lake. The pine, conifer-ridden landscape stood a good fifty-feet above where the lake crashed into the side of the bluff. It was a cliffed bit of park, headed west on it was going away from town. They supposed it would have been easier to drive all the way to their storage shed but were paranoid. Things had been upside down lately. It was best to dodge through the woods and be unseen, unknown.

They beat with the wind to their backs, ducking, dodging thickets. Twigs on the ground were carefully plotted, avoided. They burst through the wooded area and onto the cliff overlooking Lake Eerie. It was an abyss; it reminded Ben of swimming within his mind and himself, being lost, and shuddered. The trees swayed, but Ben did not feel any wind. In their dark uniforms they hugged the shadows, flowing westward. Hank broke away from Ben, and then Hec. They liked to fan out and regroup. The three of them hit an imaginary wall and turned south, plunging into the forest. They were all separate, though together—wolfpack is what we're going for.

The only problem was the terrain before them; it was a surprisingly dangerous task, getting to the cleared encamping of the mini-storage facility--'only thing mini about our storage is our prices!'

There was a mile and a half before them, containing a not so easily scaled cliffside, and a river that was wide and fast, it dumped off into a gorge at least two hundred feet deep, maybe a half mile wide. It was no joke. There happened to be an old railroad track bridging over the gorge, tho, rickety and only oft inspected. However it was also usually traveled by the train companies as it was the only way into town for them.

The water ran well below Salem in a silently humming stream as he took his first step onto the bridge, looking down. The river lay three-hundred feet below him but he could still hear it. The night was around him, if a train came at this exact moment he'd have no choice but to jump. Around him was truly a drop if there ever were one. Below was blackness but that pulsing water could be heard, sound enough. Wind blew the trees, tho barely, Ben could hear it all: in-sync, alive.

Birdie looked all around and down into the little valley, where the rabbits hopped and bugs chirped and there was the steady rustling of wind. Why couldn't life be like a nap off in the woods by a waterfall? Like a rabbit in a state park?

Fuck, Birdie thought. "Hank," he said.

"What?" Hank was in the back.

"Let me see those grapple guns."

Hank obliged, handing over the spring powered groping ropes to Bird. A section of track was struck out from the track. Bird looked over the edge of it and saw the crumbling remains of disintegrated rock, mangled steel. Hank and Ben backed up, so did Bird, who needed a running to start. He got one, jumped, and had his rope grabbing somewhere on the bridge. He swung down, back up, and landed, like a metronome. One could even call it surgical. Bird just swung, let go, landed, over a one hundred-footed gap.

44.

"Fuck," Rye grunted, lifting open the storage door, "Birdie, grab yours and go get the kid. Hitch and Heather should be leaving now, headed here."

"We know where they're headed," Salem chipped, "do you like her codename? I was thinking it should Brickhouse."

"Fuck you," Birdie said, emerging with his dirtbike. He swung over it, further muttering musings as he catapulted into the night, leaving soft dust behind him: 'set up your own joke much?', 'sell a book retard,' 'hows that new novel coming?'

The bike sped off and then did a U-turn, Rye started laughing; Bird had gone the wrong way in his anger. He wheeled around and rolled by with the bird flipped at Salem.

"Of all things that kid could've taken, he had to take the Termintator droid," Salem said, shaking his head, "funny, how shit comes together sometimes."

"Benjamin, get your damn bike off the rack. We don't have time for sentimental bullshit." Rye let his engine purr in to the dead of night, the crickets quieting for a tick, "shouldn't Hitch be here by now?"

"No, not for another twenty minutes or so," Salem replied, going under the door, moments later emerging again with the bike in tow.

Rye mounted his bike and tore up the grass, Salem did, too, the two of them jaunting off in different directions.

45

They were there grunting, struggling, biting, duct-taped like a spiderweb to the green peeling seats on the schoolbus, still in their cheerleader uniforms. Most of them hadn't even come to yet, but upfront and driving was the man everyone had been talking about. They all knew it. He started to laugh, turned around to them, "all I had to fucking do was hang out in the middle of town??!! ahahaha," he reached back and slapped one of the struggling girls, "stop that!! I don't want you bruised when we ram the prison. You ever been raped by a skinhead, sugar?" He cooed even more wildly. Facing back to the road, headlights approaching him.

46.

Heather was not so far behind the school bus now. She was practically on top of it as she downshifted again to ball passed the monstrosity. Faces peered at her from the windows, pleading desperation. She pushed, pulling ahead of the bus, the highway was three lanes wide.

Heather drove on, still not honking, thinking of what to do: one wrong move and she was dead; she knew it. Hector tried squeezing into her head but she dismissed the thought, all he'd do now is distract her. A grin flecked over her face, she considered the irony of training in the martial arts for a lifetime only to be called upon here, now. The stars looked reverent in their distance, still glowing, bringing the night light and beauty through her windshield. Time and its relevance railed through her big dumb brain when,

HONK, she honked, furiously. The schoolbus did, too. Heather half-panicked, slammed on her breaks. She thought the bus would stop to, but it did not and came barreling on her like a comet.

Now

The bus was practically on her, she brought the engine to life and weaved over to the middle lane. A stickered sport utility vehicle drove by, honking its curses. 'Drive Safely You Fucking Idiot,' and 'Use Your Blinker, Cunt,' were a couple of the fun things being yelled at them from a bumper sticker. It disappeared off down the highway. She honked again. Hitch sprung out of the trunk.

In his hands, a miniature, many-toothed, shark killer. A handheld teethed spike that was at least a foot and one half. Hitch wasted no time pulling the trigger, burying the spike into the bus.

Hitch was smart, but for whatever reason hadn't seen it coming: the wild-haired man hitting the breaks; the gun was still in his hands and he was yanked from the car.

Heather heard a *thumfk* and assumed the weapon was planted.

once you hear the speer go in, count to two, floor it. Hitch had said, *then continue to five, flip the switch.*

One

Heather accelerated, furiously,

two,

she felt them pulling away.

She flipped the switch just as Hitch was calling out to her, he was screaming 'APRICOT!!' their assigned safe-word to shut it down. Heather knew she heard him begin to scream it as the explosion also chimed in.

The bus flipped, Heather saw it happen. It flipped right over and landed on Hitch, or rather what remained of him, his guts were all there on the street. When it happened a fly away side-mirror knocked her half to a concussion.

The man with the long black hair got out, tarred from the waist up, shook the glass off himself, touched his toes, stretched a little in a few other ways, and flipped Heather the bird before running off down the highway, wild-armed.

She couldn't fathom chasing after him, herself, as she was still heavily concussed, and could feel herself slipping towards certain death. It felt like continuity. How the hell was *He* still standing, let alone galloping and tramping down the asphalt.

The screaming pulled her back from the concussion.

The girls came pouring out, Heather ran for them. Strapped to their persons with duct taped were clikcing, ticking, time

190

bombs. The sirens wailed, bore nearer still. Heather saw them but did not stop running for the girls, even when the bombs went off. She was close enough to be thrown back and then dragged along the concrete. Through the high-pitched hum in her ears she thought she heard a helicopter chug by, lake bound. Also familiar was the sound of a vehicle pulling up beside her, tho her hearing was fading, she heard the doors open, the flick of a lighter, and a familiar voice between short breathes, "jeezus christ, get her on the truck before the fuzz get here."

Hands hard as stone lifted her--the blood rushed, she was out.

47.

Jesus, is this where we left off? With god knows what happening with everything. When did it all become such a mess?

George Hammer unloaded Heather's limped body from his criminally long car, or rather his body man did.

"Hank said he was sending her and the boy away."

"I know what he said you fuckin' meathead I was there too. Obviously there was some miscommunication."

"Maybe he lied to you."

"Or maybe there was a little miscommunication, either way she's here. Why are you always calling people liars? When has Hank ever lied to us; is that not his schtick?"

"What?"

"Is that, not his schtick? You know, his prerogative? What the mother lives by. Everything that is Hank."

"Oh, I don't know. You've never introduced us."

"Shut the fuck up," George laughed. He looked at Heather, she was still warm boned, though barely breathing. "What are we to do with you?"

George's phone chirped up, he put it up to his ear, "He did what?" George had a cigar in his mouth, an angry snarl across his face. "That little shit. I told him not to fuck with my men...don't give me that bullshit...he knew the guards were off limits. Fucking dick." George hung up the call and squatted on a stump. His body man stood over Heather, who was tied up to a tree, about four feet from the ground; she was coming to every now and again. The moonlight longened the wooded shadows, a dirt road and the lake were nearby.

George loosened the collar on his shirt and took off his tie, listened to the waves beat on some barren skirt of cliff. "Humpty dumpty," he said to himself.

"What?" said his bodyman.

"Humpty Dumpty," George said, wiping sweat from his half haired, penis-shaped, head, "they never tell you which side of the wall he fell to."

48.

"Chief, we've got something." Officer Chip Gregory always opened doors over-aggressively, today called for such haste. The office phones rang behind him and off in the corner men crowded around a map. The news of Asher's death had, of course, broke. Along with that came the tape in his office, they'd already recovered Hannah Storm's body from her apartment, found no clues save for a few long hairs.

A balding man sat behind a desk with a cigarette burning on the lip of his ashtray. He wore his holsters and a long sleeved shirt made of strong and durable material. He had nice shoes, too.

"Fuck, tell me it's good, Chip." Chief Brent said, seeming five years older than he had two weeks ago. His mustache was usually tamed but it looked like a shrub run wild.

"He killed all the guards at the jail."

"Fuck," Brent picked up his cigarette and took a hit. "I'm assuming he let the degenerates go?"

"It didn't seem like he let anyone go. By the time we got there all the inmates were in their cells. Though they were all quiet, so quiet. It's funny, I knew they were all behind bars but that silence was unnerving."

"That's not funny, Chip."

"Yeah, no. But then we checked the manifest and he let one guy out. Ulman."

"Ulman?" The Chief stroked his mustache and thought. "That doesn't make any sense."

"You know him?"

"No. And that's why it doesn't make any sense. I figured he'd let out a big-timer. Grady, or Batch. One of those other sickos."

"Ulman was taken into custody last year, not from here. He works for the Circus. Let a tiger loose on one of his rape victims."

"One of them?"

"Yeah. Just a guess but I doubt she was the first."

Smoke floated and hung in the air. Chief Brent listened to the bustle about him for a moment. "So Ulman's the only one he took?"

"Yeah, we went over everything. Tried interviewing the other inmates but like I said they were all silent. They all just stared like we weren't there."

"Fuck what is going on, anyway? I always knew those trapeezing, painted, fucking mutants were up to something. What's going on out there?" The chief put out his cigarette and looked out his door the best he could. Commotion stood outside of it. "Did any of those girls on the bus survive?"

"No, chief."

Chief Brent looked out again, "shit," he said under his breath.

"Chip," a man said, entering the room. "You look awful. Swine flu?"

"Nice fuckin' leotard, Rye." Chief Brent addressed the costumed man. "What the fuck are you doing here? You're still on the wanted list."

"And Bigfoot is still roaming around out there."

"Rye,"

"I'm not done. The G spot is also easily found."

"Jesus, this is serious."

"Really? Then why was Officer Johnson over there looking at porn?"

"Fuck," Brent stood up and went to close his door, "Johnson stop watching your torture porn on the job you fucking ingrate! I'm going to have Rye here chop your balls off." The door slammed, and with it the sound of the station was dulled. "You have something? We figured you guys would have split after Asher outted you."

"Yeah," Rye said, giving the Chief a queer look "he broke into the jail and is probably headed…"

"For the Circus, yes I know. Chip just told me the same. Now, can we go to the circus already?"

"Birdie is on his way. I came to get you guys."

"Vamos!" The Chief said, throwing on his coat and reopening the door, "andale!" The office went quiet, everyone peaked up and looked at the chief. "Let's go, people, circus. Double time."

The officers all looked around, confused. One of them off in the corner spoke up. "The circus?"

"Sherlock!" Brent yelled, "get your gun, put on your jacket, and let's go to the circus."

"Should we get our car keys too, Chief?" Another one asked.

"Yes! What the fuck, Chuck. Let's go. Set up a perimeter yada yada, you all know the drill."

"Rousing speech, Chief," Rye said, still in the office with Chip.

"Shut the fuck up, Hank." The chief said quietly, "you get out of here before I have one of these fucktards arrest you. When this is done you're all going to be held accountable. I'm still not so sure that it wasn't *you* who killed Asher after he told everyone who you were." When the chief turned back around Rye was gone, Chip pointed to the window. The whole of Trident's finest got their shit and made for the Circus.

49.

"....and last is Salem, or young Ben Paradise. His father was Bud Paradise, who died some years ago as part of the vigilante group, himself, if you all remember when Brock Opti hosted a massacre over at the elementary school. Now that we have name's out of the way, I urge that we seek peace and understanding. So, tonight at ten pm I am requesting, and indeed inviting, everyone to the studio here to meet with me. Heroes, villains...cops, all of you out there, too, citizens. We do best together, shining in the light. All of you need to turn yourselves in. No one can live up and above the law, even if it's perceived as 'good.' So ten pm, here at NewsNet Two. I implore you come."

50

He began to laugh like a sick and invalid hyena. Like an insane leper who'd just killed Jesus. His hair swung heavily, unwashed and oil soaked. Behind him was a man in chains. "Who are you?" asked the man. It was probably the twentieth time he'd asked the question. At first he'd gotten no response. Now all he got were laughs.

"Your mother, bitch," said the gangly, black painted weirdo, laughing again. "Your mother bitch," he repeated, howling, pleased with his own joke. "I'm your cockandballs, motherfucker."

They were both in a field. A long, moonlit, field running along the Lake. They were walking east. A large tent rose up in front of them, the nylon flaps draped around gleamed in the full light of the moon. Obviously one of the bounding fools was the villain our heroes have been after. The other was a bald and sharp-nosed chap of about forty-five. His face was rough but not in an entirely unkind way. His eyes seemed to sulk, but not for himself, rather humanity, or for existence, or the futility in it. Whatever it was hanging there left him utterly uncaring for much of anything. He was a human dud. He'd found the truth: nothing meant anything so what all was it anyway. He was utterly disgusted with effort. "If you are going to kill me just do it," he said, dully.

"Don't you think I would have?" A quick slap to the face woke the bald man back from his skulk.

"No. You play silly little games. I'd think you to patter me around awhile first."

"Shut up, Ulman." He slapped Ulman one more time, yanking his chain and dropping him to the ground, "I could take a shit on you right now if I wanted. I could sodomize you, I could pee in your mouth…"

"Patter patter," Ulman said, getting back on his feet. "I don't suppose you are going to tell me what this is all about?"

"It really all started when my death was faked, my father killed. Someone I considered my friend then ganged up with the people who killed my father."

"What?" Ulman continued walking, chain-bound, very confused. "You make no sense,"

"THEY FUCKING KILLED HIM," the man screamed, "AFTER HE LET ME FREE!!!" He went nuts, started scratching himself, pulling his hair, running and diving into the ground. A real weirdo.

Ulman collected himself, familiar with the unstable. "Everyone has their reasons you know." It was always ironic to Ulman that these insane men could often be clicked back in with a simple line of understanding. Not this one. Ulman thought maybe he'd never actually seen a man who'd truly lost it.

"He did what he should have. He helped me and they killed him for it."

Ulman had no idea what the man was talking about. Before he knew what to do the pair were approaching the tents of a ringed circus, closed for the evening, but still with strange happenings about. Ulman kept his head up for anyone familiar, but saw no one. Tho, he heard and smelled the tigers almost at once. Surely they felt his return as well. This motherfucker was crazy if he thought himself to be the most dangerous person here, even tho Ulman was in chains...."what do you intend to do about it?"

"ha," the painted man giggled a bit, "kill them. I took you so they would follow me here." The stranger became more animated, using his hands, "you were the only one really and truly sick who was locked up from the circus, they'd have to come here."

"What if they don't," Ulman heard purring in his ear, they'd approached a tent, he'd need only to distract this sucker, his tigers lay two tents away, near the cliffed-edge, over-looking the lake. The tent they entered held a caged-lion.

"They will," He said, "hold it," he stopped Ulman and they both stood outside of the tent by a few dozen feet. "It's ten pm." Off in the distance explosions could be heard.

"Jesus,"

"Says the rapist,"

Sirens could be heard out there, only who knows where they were going. He bolted, away from Ulman. The balding man tried to get with him but fell because of his chains, he heard one of his tigers howl in pain and then the other growl. Ulman fought to get up, between tents, listening to cries of pain, but he kept getting dragged around. His face ran smack into a tent post, his teeth caught on wire. He sat there on his knees, went to get up and fell again. "No!" he yelled.

"Who the fuck are you?"

"Wha?" Ulman turned around and there was a kid-sized, well, kid in costume, approaching him from the west, past a few tents.

"Answer me," the kid was on him now, bent to one knee, tilting his head.

Ulman recognized the uniform now that he was close, "recruiting you a little young, eh?" He said to the stranger.

201

"Who are you?"

"Sh..."

"Why?"

Another cry of pain erupted from the tent where the tigers were housed. Ulman winced.

"Is he in there?" The kid still had a kid's voice, Ulman thought he could not be older than 10.

"Yes," said Ulman, suddenly feeling tired, "stop him, please. He's....killing my tigers."

The kid brought his boot to the man's head, tho cut the chain he was bound to. "I know who you are, fuckface," he brought his foot up again and Ulman slumped over, out cold. Laughter was heard a few tents down. Of course, context being what it is we know the kid to be Theo Matthis, hot on the trail of his mother's killer. The fear Theo should have felt was replaced and overwhelmed with rage. That fucking freak would get his. Theo stood up and looked over the lake, to his left. The wind went ahead and softened the night. The moon looked close and shone bright. A few paces ahead of Theo loomed a tent, large and red. The young man was not inclined for the want to feel fear but felt it still, What time was it? He'd wanted to end this before it got too late, there was something sinister living in the dead of night and Theo would rather not see that culminate with whatever his nemesis had in store. The tent flaps blew easily, opening enough for Theo to see the blackness within.

Theo sat, took off his mask, thinking a minute and taking it all in, contemplating on how to proceed. He could still ditch and run; it was not too late. 'yes it is,' he said to himself. 'and fuck this guy anyway.' He rocked a bit then stood up, getting out his knife. He walked towards where the flaps bore him entrance, nodding to himself, confirming his belief in the plan, sweaty palmed. He veered just right of the entrance and approached the rope staking the tent up and to the ground, cutting it. The tent barely gave; Theo wandered around to the next one. The next rope was hidden between tents, in a small ten foot vacuum of blackness, where the moon's light did not reach because of the closeness of the tents. It looked like a small cave to Theo. He was sure the man he was after might lie in wait, this was a clever sonofabitch. Theo held his breath and dove in, finding the rope by feel and slashing it. He ran while he did so, emerging back into the moonlight, there was an explosion south, towards the city; Theo wondered and hoped help was still coming. He slashed the rope just in front of him and the tent really began to give.

"You know why she had to die, don't you?" Theo heard someone talking to him, under the quickly collapsing pile of nylon.

Theo remained quiet. He'd not play along. He was sick of it. Realizing he was holding a pattern he did a 180 and began walking back around the tent from where he'd just came, dodging under the dark spot between tents with ease, there was nothing threatening in them with Him around the other side. Something made Theo stop, he did so. Listening. He put his ear up to the tent and heard the rough breathe of a large animal. He put his hand where the body of the beast was, tho he was on the wrong side to touch it. He listened a moment longer, awe-stricken. Something moved on the other side and Theo heard a terrible yelp, then silence. His hand was still up and he felt the beast go limp. This guy was toast. Theo reached into his pack, pulled out four medium sized pods. He circled the tent and put them on the ground, spaced evenly. He then hit a button, making the tent go up like the empire state building. The pods beamed spotlights around the pitch, maggot had nowhere to run. Theo cut the remaining three ties down, it all held. Of course.

203

"What did you think would happen?" The voice mocked, within. Another blast went off, this one further away. *Fuck, where was the cavalry, surely they'd put it together by now,* flashed in Theo's mind. A definite breeze pushed in from the lake, making the flaps on the tent go nuts. He'd just have to do it. He stood there and waited a minute, hoping it would all implode; it did not. He drew breathe, clicked on the light sitting on his pack, pulled a flap back and immersed himself, the lights he'd set up useless behind the opaque nylon draws. However, his flashlight was quite useful, a little LED thing cleverly designed to flash and distract if needed. Tho, He was nowhere. There were, however, two tigers, one dead and one who may as well have been. Theo could tell the dead one was the one he'd been touching outside, given the direction. But the room was fairly empty with few true corners. No one else was there. Theo turned out his light and listened. A school bus started up. Theo ran, booked it, he'd dove out just before the bus rammed into the tent, over the already dead tiger. The tigress on the opposite side tried to keep her eyes open amid bouts with consciousness, licking her wounds. Light flooded in from the foreground. Theo was just outside and saw him get off the bus. There was a dirt bike out there, Theo heard it clearly. Followed by the scream of a woman. As the bike drew on Theo knew He would be waiting for a distraction; Theo was intent with his conviction. The bike sounded off again, Theo realizing his mother's murderer was put off by it, so much so that he began to sprint away, tho he hooked, seemingly to circle around.....

51

Bird gripped his bike, risking steep crossings and sharp turns, trees, he felt confident with the bike Hitch had built for him. The engine ran in quick succession and the suspension was finely tuned. He got over Indian Bluff, then cut down a beaten dirt path, heading towards town. He'd need to navigate nearly three miles of mildly wooded terrain but Bird was a finely tuned super hero, himself, a true professional. He relished the opportunity, in fact. He turned on the police scanner, something would come up, it always had. The news of Asher's death along with the paint found in his office led everyone else to believe that the freak had struck again. However, a certain homicidal drone had exploded just down and out the window of the newsroom. It was Theo. Bird grunted, some good that info would do, 'gee we knew where he was two and a half hours ago.' Where had he run to?

"Bird, I'm back," Salem rang in Hector's ear. He'd made it back to the HUB in Hitch's home. Of course, Hitch lives in the upstairs portion of his house, but the bottom floor was another story. There was clutter jammed up, blocking the windows. The occupants of the bottom floor to Hitch's home looked to be total slobs who used their entire space as a dumpster. However, the garbage was piled up to conceal the computer, and the audio-visual equipment room that was the HUB. Salem had maps at his disposal, computers, a phone, police scanner, couch, even the launch pad to a missile silo out in the country. Were the world ending Salem would only need hit a button and a missile containing human DNA and various forms of information on us and our way of life would shoot out to space. Music, diagrams, etc..."Rye went over to the prison outside of town....He was there." Bird's police scanner clicked in, mashing radio waves at first but then a clear, *'attention all units attention all units, 401 in process, that's right all hands on deck. Perp is the painted killer and he is known to be at the circus grounds. 2400 County Road. Report there and see your superior officer for further instructions.'*

"Salem?"

"Yeah I heard it,"

"Well,"

"Are you sure he'll be there?""

"Who, Theo?"

"Yeah"

"Yeah, I have a feeling," Bird emerged by the university entrance just on the outskirts of town, the quaint buildings of businesses, firms, could be seen down the road but Bird's dirt path came out in front of the on-campus bike trail: amid trees and brick buildings. Cathedral-like atonements of learning led on around town as a kind of educational shell. Bird hung behind a few trees. He was making sure his boots were strapped tight.

"Bird," Salem rang again in his ear, just before the explosion. It obliterated the Library and cafe building in the middle of the student housing block. Birdie was frightened, he was not expecting it. "Bird," Salem said again, "that explosion was the second, there was another one at Newsnet."

"Shit,"

"Make for the circus, get Theo,"

"I have to help,"

"Hank and I are going to help, get Theo. We'll be over there soon as we can."

"I'll be there in fifteen,"

Bird went off, the circus was pushed by the lake. He had a straight shot, along the shore, it was probably eight miles, brrrp,rrp,rp,rp,brrrp,...and so on, it kicked and vibrated in his clutching thighs.

"Hector," Salem sounded grave.

"Yeah,"

"We don't know where Heather or Hitch are. Everything went upside down on us, still is,"

"Shit, alright,they never made it to Charlie?"

"Negative,"

"Alright, shit, maybe they got the drop on the Circus," Bird went on, the soft glow of a fire loomed a bit ahead, just along the shore. He killed his engine, everything went quiet for a moment.

"I feel like they would have at least checked in," Salem went on, of course they would have.

"Hold on,"

"What?"

"There's a fire pitched out here, in nowheresland. I'm gonna check it out before I go buzzing by."

"Alright, I've got your coordinates. Let me know; I'm going to be around the HUB for a minute."

It made sense. The fire out there, however, did not. Bird got out his birdnoculars and adjusted them for focus. What he saw was a very large man, looking through his own binoculars, and directly at Bird. Next to him was the ever chode-like George Reginald Hammer; taped to a tree was Heather. What the fuck. The big guy said something to George, both parties did not want to be the first to break. Bird pondered, Heather wasn't bleeding, she was alive; she could be dead, but she wasn't. Hector pulled down his specs, casually got back onto his bike, "Hammer has Heather," he said to Salem,

"What?"

"Hammer, and his pet gorilla."

"Oh. Hitch?"

An explosion went off, not very close but still enough to shake the earth a bit. "No Hitch," Bird gunned it, hoping they'd be distracted enough for him to gain some kind of ground. A second explosion. "I'm going for her."

"duh," Salem laughed on the other end, "isn't that your schtick?"

Birdie got close enough to see Hammer scurrying about, it looked like they were they were trying to cut Heather down, he was closing the gap. His mind's eye saw how it would time up and he got chills; it was going to work. He cut his headlight, thirty paces now, "WHAT ARE YOU FUCKING IDIOTS DOING?!" Bird yelled. He was on the camp now, and was still full-throttle, he must have been doing forty. Hammer was running for the truck and his man abandoned cutting down Heather. He'd almost had her, but turned instead to try and punch Bird straight from his seat. He was much too late. Birdie jumped from the bike and it slammed George's guy, pinning him to a tree. Bird finished cutting down heather in a literal flash and wielded her in one arm, lept over and grabbed his bike with the other. George was pulling around, drew his firearm. Heather was fashioned to be slumped on the seat, hugging him. Bird kicked as George came around, yanked on the throttle, speeding east. George's truck was facing west. "Don't you fucking do it, Hammer!" Bird yelled, gunning past the truck. "Don't you fucking shoot at me!!" He went on,

George did not. Instead he grabbed his body man from the ground, placing him in the trunk bed, and made for the hospital. Heather stirred, The Circus was only another mile up. Bird could feel it now, coming to a draw. "Heather," he said. Her eyes opened and she began screaming, panicking, Bird almost got dumped down the cliff and into the lake. She shrieked with the force of a thousand succubi. "Woah!" Bird grabbed her and the bike tight as he could, a boa could not have done a better job. "It's Hec," he said.

"Hitch," she sobbed, pounding Hector on the back. "Hitch."

"Fuck," Bird felt vomit want to come up and out.

"We thought we had Him," Heather continued crying into Hector's chest as he drove. Their silhouettes blurred over the edged cliff, and the moon beyond the lake. They drew nearer, the tents could be seen clearly, there and red....

52

'You know me, too.' Someone said in Theo's head. It sounded most ironically like the AI ridden voice the drone carried within him. However, Theo could feel something behind it all, a true presence. 'My other friend is out there, dying.'

Theo thought, his man still sprinting away, down the coast line. He wanted to howl, this man could not go. Theo could not catch him, only being twelve. The tigress in his head still hung, trying to understand. Theo pulled up his gun and shot a couple times, completely missing, hearing the painted man laugh as he sprant away, taunting all the while. The tiger latched on to his brain like the drone had, Theo came to: 'why all the distractions? So I can hear a tiger in my head? Does that change what I am trying to do? The only resounding answer Theo could muster up was, 'no!'

The dirtbike only gained ground, it sounded close, he figured Bird and probably Heather. They'd come to drag him out of this. Theo heard a great roar and the large, clawed beast leapt from its bed. wounds licked, she set her course and bound the painted freak. Theo watched in awe. The orange of her was such a blur, he'd no idea an animal could move that quickly. Especially such a large one. She was gone; He had no chance. When she reached Him she slashed His hamstring, Theo saw His leg rip open, He crumpled; she left him like that, then sat next to him and licked his blood. The man screamed until he passed out. Theo suddenly realized the gangly asshole was not so important, malicious, or anything. He was a screaming and squirming man until He was a meal. He was no monster; He was a little bitch. Theo laughed, got up, grabbed his glock, he couldn't contain himself. He was elated, sanctified: what was there to fear, anyway? Who the fuck did this asshole think he was? His tigress grabbed Him by the neck, dropped Him a few feet from Theo who walked up to Him. He was painted, of course, stupid haired. It was obvious his neurons had been neglected. Theo raised it up, breathing, hearing Bird behind him, screaming, approaching quickly. He was saying, "no!" but fuck that, fuck. that. It ends. He pulled his finger and surprised himself with how well he handled the recoil. He spun around, shot at the tires of the dirt bike, tiger still sitting by. Nothing landed but still it skidded and tumbled, Heather and Hec tumbled too and then got up. Theo faced them, gun in hand. He pulled his finger twice more and Heather dropped. "How many people have to die for you, Hec?" He laughed, waving the gun about as if he were counting everyone up, 'you, you, you?'

"Theo," Hector was defeated; he didn't know what to do. Madness was the special anymore. "don't, man." He dropped, "don't give in," Hector sat there, Theo too, "it can stop right now. He's dead."

With the tigress came a sense and a taste for the savage side of life. Theo felt like some in-tuned Navajo who'd somehow ran head first and soul into a tiger; he pulled the trigger, Hector slumped. "I know you are why she had to die, when it comes down to it," Theo spat on Bird and his uniform, picked up the dirtbike, and sped off, the tiger close enough, following at its own pace. Jazz music was over the lake. Jazz music in b minor.

Just like that it was done.

AFTERWARD

The walls glowed a red hue, the stone hearth stood before the flames, also illuminated: red. Hank sat in his great chair, the kind you see old Nazi psychologists sit in while smoking a cigar. The room was great, the fireplace itself, hand-carved. He could hear them all outside honking their horns tho it only came as a muffle. Their shouts were faint and could barely beat through the walls of Hank's mansion. He had on his bathrobe, was slumped: what was he to do? It was night and the villagers had come for him. The soft glow of their torches bounced off the lake.

When they'd started to mob Hank retreated to a room far back in to his house. It would take most people fifteen minutes to find it.

Hank stood up and went over to a crystal bottle, poured its brown liquid in to a crystal glass, did not bother with ice, and sighed as he went to sit back down: brushing his hair back with one hand. He stoked the fire.

"Sir,"

"Yes, Butler, come in."

"Very good sir but I think you should come with me, they've fetched ladders and are beginning to scale the walls."

"What do they want, me dead?"

"They are outraged, sir, their intent could be to kill you or simply give you a good berating."

"So I'm supposed to run?" Hank took a hit, "fat chance. I'm sitting here in my own house. My god damn dick is still just swinging around in this robe and I'm supposed to answer for everything. God dammit." He threw the glass at a wall, "I'm

213

the only one left! Time to have me drawn and quartered, I suppose."

"Theo may still be out there."

"Yeah." Hank slumped back in to his chair. "But they'll burn the city down." He thought. "You go."

"Sir?"

"You, go, get him to safety and all that. If I'm still alive I'll find you. Maybe."

"Sir,"

"go, take as much money as you need. Take enough to retire. I don't give a fuck." Hank was practically mumbling, looking down at the ground. "Get the fuck out of here."

Butler turned, stopped, "will that be all, sir?"

"Jesus fuck Butler go! Leave me to the wolves."

"Very we…."

"Wait, get me another drink."

Butler obliged, bid Hank with a nod, and slipped off down a corridor.

It only took a few minutes for their shouts to echo through his walls: 'THERE'S A FIRE DOWN THIS WAY!' there were flashlights, torches, Hank saw them flashing towards and then away from him. Hank took a breathe, downed his drink, the voices were drawing nearer still. He laughed to himself, shook his head. Drawing himself up, he approached a bookshelf, pulling a book off. He flipped through a few pages before the shelf disappeared behind a wall, revealing a staircase. Shouts of 'DOWN HERE, DOWN HERE, I SEE A SHADOW!' combined with the flashlights and torches, they were on him. The flood of light was making waves down the hall. Hank ascended the stairs, flicked the wall shut behind him. The mob entered and saw an empty room, save for a book on the floor. That was the trick with trick bookcases, make them to be used only one time, then people cannot follow.

Up Hank climbed, and quickly, they couldn't technically open the door but with a pick axe and a strong enough man....there were enough people there for one of them to go, 'LET'S SEE WHAT'S BEHIND THE BOOKCASE. YARRRRRR.'

There were another twenty or so steps before him and all was still quiet down below. Then he heard it.

TING TING

The sound of metal on stone clanged through the narrow staircase, it pierced Hank's ears. No matter, Hank met the landing up in his tower. He jumped up, closed and padlocked the door. It was six inches of titanium and completely pick-axe proof. They'd need to blow the door with sticks of dynamite to get to him.

The lake sat well below the tower, Hank turned and approached the spot where he did not build a wall, but a plank, it jutted out a good twenty feet from the tower. There was a black suit hung on a wall to his left, he grabbed it and put it on. It was a full body wingsuit and Hank zipped it up, raised his arms to see if it still fit correctly. He took a breathe, then another, started flapping around the tower like a bird, 'you can do this,' he said it over and over again. At some point the urge hit him like a wall and he thought it best not to double think the inspiration. He began to sprint from the tower, gaining ground and running across the plank, Hank caught just a glimpse of what was below him before he jumped and dive bombed towards it. The rocks below, the water hurtling in to them. He breathed, at ease, remembering the practice, his training. It may have been awhile but this was ca....he opened his arms, legs, slowly rolled in to a full on bullet racing across the lake. Splitting the stone pillars, he was gone.

Dear Reader,

I am glad you've made it this far. Being a young writer has granted me nothing but stress and some really shitty decision making; it's great. I have to look around, watch language die and books get reduced to one of two things: 'I study historical symbols and it's going to save America,' or 'here is my interpretation of how you can improve your well-being.' There is not one laugh to be had in any of that fucking dribble, hardly a cry either besides the sound of our souls dying. So, if you can't find any pot--or even if you can--curl up with this book, or my next one. Learn how to read if you have to. We are in a new age and it calls for new rules. There is still room on this planet for a well-placed word or two and it is evident by how many people are reading books on the 'L' train.

Bring me your dissatisfied and unentertained; I will give them prose they will laugh at and then say, 'that wasn't funny.'

We are all hypocrites who hate the bad things we think we see in ourselves.

I hope you enjoyed the book. Until next time...

Cleveland, Ohio
August, 2018

"I take you as the personification of evil, as the destroyer of the soul, as the maharanee of the night. Tak your womb to my wall, so that I may remember you. We must get going. Tomorrow, tomorrow…."

Shane Goulette is a writer from Cleveland, Ohio. This is his second work, following up his first project of short stories and poems 'Chickens Don't Fart: A Bunch of Nonsense.' While not represented, or formally published, Shane has written and published two books, with plans on writing more.

Made in the USA
Middletown, DE
07 October 2018